GUARDED

There are secrets;
and then there are secrets that kill.

An Inspirational Historical Romance

Novel by Award Winning Author

Eva Maria Hamilton

Bible quotes taken from the New King James Version.

Cover Design by Eva Maria Hamilton

This is a work of fiction. Names, characters, places, and incidents, are either the product of the author's imagination or are used fictitiously, and any resemblance to actual persons, living or dead, business establishments, events or locales is entirely coincidental.

ISBN: 978-1-0689907-2-4

http://www.LilacLanePublishing.com

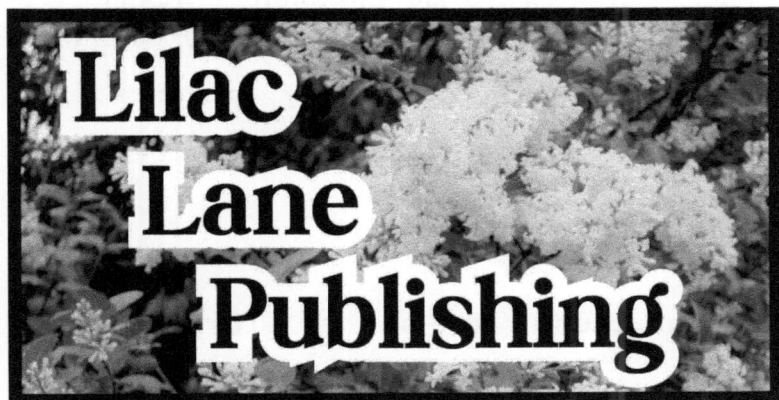

Dedicated with love to my family,
especially my husband, Jason;
daughters, Michelina and Angelina;
collies, Daisy and Glory; parents, Bob
and Lina; and brother, Bill.

For these, and all my blessings, I
thank God.

My little children, let us not love in
word, neither in tongue; but in deed
and in truth. 1 John 3:18

The Mohawk Valley, New York State, USA

Saturday, July 10, 1813

During the War of 1812

Blair McAllister hurled the door of the general store open, his eyes glued to the scene on the street before him. A woman chased her bonnet in the middle of the road, unable to see a wagon that charged recklessly down an intersecting lane.

He dropped his farm supplies. They crashed onto the sidewalk behind him as his feet pounded the compacted earth. The woman froze when the wagon turned the corner and hastened straight for her.

As he neared her, the dust from the horses' hooves clouded over them. "Run." He shoved the woman forward, leaving himself to scramble out of the wagon's path. *Please, God, don't let me die. Elsie needs me.*

He braced himself. But nothing threw him off his feet. Coughing, he looked past the haze, as the wagon clamored down the road.

"Are you injured?" He stepped toward the woman who swatted dirt off her empire waist gown.

"Nay." Her face compressed.
"I—I—I—" she sneezed "—I'm fine."
She finally met his eyes, and he
beheld the bluest skies within them.
Then she bent down and picked up her
lacy bonnet. After several slaps to
rid the material of dust she tilted
her face up to him. "Were you harmed?"

He shook his thirty year old head
whilst rubbing the soil off the front
of his formerly white shirt. "I'm no
worse for wear." The woman nodded then
turned a frown upon herself.
Obviously, being covered in a layer of
earth didn't please her. Not that
anything would have deterred from her
beauty one iota.

He raked a hand through his hair
to suppress his laughter. He doubted
this woman had ever gotten dirty. Her
floor-length gown wasn't made of the
less expensive linsey-woolsey material
most lasses wore, or even calico, this
woman wore silk. And the color matched
her eyes impeccably.

He whacked his trousers. Aside
from the shopkeeper, he knew of not
one other single man who knew the
distinction between those fabrics, but

since he'd become the sole guardian of his sister's daughter, that wee lass had taught him a multitude of things he hadn't previously known.

"You're certain I didn't injure you?" He appraised the beautiful blonde-haired woman. "If I pushed you overly hard, I apologize."

"You needn't apologize. I assure you, I'm fine." She twisted her fancy white bonnet between shaky fingers. "I ought to be thanking you for saving my life." She glanced at him. "Please, excuse me. I'm somewhat distraught and my manners have eluded me."

He dipped his chin with a smile. "I understand." His senses were also askew. However, his hadn't been affected by the near accident, his were tattered because of her—the sweetness of her lips, the prettiness of her face—he simply could not take his eyes off her. She was strikingly beautiful.

Nevertheless, he rubbed the back of his neck, he couldn't just stand there gawking at her. "I don't recall ever seeing you in town before. Are you just passing through or will you be staying?" He held his breath and hoped for the latter.

"I just came from Upper Canada. I shall be staying for some time." His heart leapt as the woman tucked loose strands of hair behind her ears.

"Then I feel 'tis my duty to inform you that this section of the road is called *Bash Bend*."

"Ah." A smile lit her eyes. "And for good reason. Henceforth, I shall avoid it."

He bowed. "I've resided here my entire life, if you require any help reaching your destination I'd be happy to oblige."

She didn't answer. She couldn't. Bystanders swarmed around them. They fussed over her with the utmost concern. In mere moments the distance between them grew to unspeakable lengths as they led her away.

Mesmerized, he continued to watch her. And a smile twitched at his lips when she looked over her shoulder. There was no mistaking the thrill that shot through him when her eyes met his. She had sought him out, and thus, he could no longer temper his grin.

"Blair?" Lachlan McAllister sang his name. "I shan't ask you *again* if you're wounded, because your heart obviously is." His cousin laughed. "You're enamored with her."

He tore his eyes away from her. "She wasn't wearing a wedding ring."

His cousin chuckled even louder as they walked back across the street. "Aye, there's not a doubt remaining—" Lachlan clapped him on the back "—you're finally smitten."

He shrugged lightheartedly. What could he say? His cousin stood absolutely correct.

"Did you ascertain her name?"

"There wasn't time. However, she did say she would be in town for a while."

"Then she shall either be at church to-morrow, or you can interrogate every parishioner until someone either tells you who she is, or better yet, offers to introduce you."

"Precisely what I had planned." He grinned, then began to collect his jumbled supplies off the sidewalk. "To-morrow cannot come fast enough."

"Hey, British lover," a drunkard's slurred words hit him as the man's fist tried to make contact with his face.

Blair grabbed the man's arm, twisted the appendage behind his back, and pushed him into the store's wall. The drunkard let out a groan as his chest hit the wood.

"If you need to voice your opinion about this war—" Blair growled into the man's ear "—then I suggest you speak to those in power, because attempting to bully me or anyone else into submission shan't work. Ever."

"This ain't over." The drunkard struggled. Blair pulled his arm tighter and shoved him harder into the wall until the man moaned but said nothing more.

"Lachlan, would you be so kind as to fetch the sheriff. I think we have someone here who could benefit from a wee reprieve from the bottle."

*   *   *

Seated in the first pew at church didn't provide Penelope Sherwood with the most advantageous place in which to view the other worshippers. But she must try. Her neck pinched when she looked over her shoulder. She rubbed the sore spot. She couldn't turn her head like that again unless she wished to deepen the pain. Getting pushed out of that wagon's line of terror yesterday had done more harm than she'd realized.

But she was grateful to the man who had saved her—the very handsome man. *Her hero*, she nearly sighed at the remembrance of his puppy dog brown eyes that had held such concern for her well-being.

Enough. She shook the romantic notions from her head. She wasn't here to find a beau. She was in this foreign land on a mission. One she took seriously. And nothing—or no one—would get in her way. She would remain focused. Forget the tall stranger with the coffee brown hair.

She folded her hands in her lap and looked up to the pulpit at her friend's father, Pastor West. She would ruminate on his words, and steel her mind not to wander back to that gentleman, even if he was the most attractive man she had ever laid eyes on.

Oh, dear. She squeezed her eyelids shut. *These thoughts will never do. God, You must help me. You are the only one who knows why I'm here. Why I swapped homes with the pastor's daughter. I came here to find P.J. I need to know he's being treated well. I couldn't bear it if her were being abused. Please, God, keep him safe and guide me to him. I need to find him and fulfill my pa's dying wish.*

"Amen," the other parishioners' final words jerked her eyes open. And even though she wanted to jump out of her seat and begin her search anew she had to wait for the others to vacate their pews ahead of her.

Finally exiting the church, she squinted into the bright sunlight and hurried to open her parasol. She mustn't lose any more time. She had to locate P.J.

But everyone had already begun to talk in groups, rendering her task of seeing anyone's face that much more difficult. She walked along the edge of the crowd to an elevated spot that offered an encompassing view of the parishioners. In the shade of a birch tree she closed her parasol then opened her fan to relieve herself from the summer's heat. However, 'twas all for naught. As she examined the crowd she didn't see P.J. Hoping for a better view she pushed up on her tiptoes.

"Are you in search of someone?" A deep voice thrust forth from behind her.

Swiftly she turned. And lost her balance. With her ankle bent at an awkward angle she fell and struck the man in the chest with her fan.

"Sorry." She looked up into the same puppy dog eyes that had appeared in her dreams the night before. She swallowed even though her mouth was dry. The man stood entirely too close as he held her elbows.

Their nearness didn't seem to bother him. He laughed and the lines that cornered his eyes crinkled with amusement. "I imagine I pushed you a wee bit harder than that yesterday, hence, I offer you a truce." He took a half step back and withdrew his hands once she'd righted herself.

Exasperated, she studied the ground under her feet as a blush crept onto her cheeks. She really was a fully capable woman of twenty-five and yet this man wouldn't know that from what he had seen of her.

"Shall we proclaim ourselves even?" the man repeated, and pulled her out of her thoughts.

She dared a look at him. "I would like nothing more, but I fail to see how we can be even."

The man's eyes grew. "You don't harbor plans to harm me further, do you?" His lips hinted at the mischievous nature of his comment. She couldn't help but stare at them.

And although she wanted to laugh along with him, her heart skipped, and she could not. However, somehow she did manage to murmur, "I didn't have any intentional plans in the matter."

"That's good to know." He laughed.

And the warmth of his smile calmed her and made her words flow more easily, "I'm indebted to you for saving my life, so I cannot comprehend how we may be even. And furthermore, I fear I haven't even expressed my full gratitude to you." She spread her fan once more. She had to do something with her nearly shaking hands. Did he know the affect he had on her? "I should have thanked you more profusely after you saved me."

The man's lips parted into a smile. "You do realize you haven't actually said *thank you* yet? You've only alluded to it."

She stared into his brown depths where a glint of folly was etched. "True." She snapped her fan closed and arched a brow. She liked his humor, and the fact that there was more to her hero than sheer attractiveness. "Thank you, kind sir." She found her nerve to exaggerate every word.

With a smirk, he dipped his chin—a very strong, masculine chin. She took a deep lungful of air and fidgeted with her fan as her eyes stayed locked on his. Had she affected him? Perhaps she had. And that caused pleasure to flood her.

Clearly, this town had more to offer than merely a place to lay her head as she completed her quest. And yet, this seemingly obvious blessing stood as anything but a blessing. Any thoughts she possessed must be focused on the attainment of her goal. This man had already distracted her for far longer than she ought to have ever allowed.

"I do believe we have a truce." She forced her eyes away from his and back to her work of looking through the crowd.

"Good." The man dipped his chin. "Now, if you'll tell me who you're searching for maybe I may offer some assistance?"

Her eyes darted back to the man beside her. She shouldn't have appeared that obvious in her quest, because 'twas completely impossible, not to mention absurd, for her to ever blurt out that she had come here in search of not only a fellow British citizen, but a British officer who had been taken to this little town in the Mohawk Valley of the United States as a prisoner of war.

"I'm merely admiring the faces of this community, seeing if there are any familiar ones."

"Then I hope you shan't mind if I join you, because as coincidental as this may seem, part of my job actually involves watching people."

She moved her eyes over the formidable looking man, from the tip of his black boots, that stuck out from under his grey drop front trousers, up past his blue fitted single-breasted tailcoat, over his white cravat, and finally to his top hat, that added more polish to his appearance.

She couldn't force this man to go away. And besides, what harm could come from spending a little more time on pleasantries with him?—as long as she kept her focus on looking for the man she had actually come to town for.

"I would have thought by your tanned skin, those rough hands of yours, and the supplies you spilled in front of the general store yesterday, that you're a farmer." She squinted at him. "And yet, I've heard of shepherds watching over sheep, but I have never heard of a shepherd paid to watch people? I think perhaps you engage it different farming practices down here."

The man chuckled and shook his head at her. "You compel me to laugh. But I have yet to repay the favor. And although my asking may be entirely improper, I simply must know your name so I may try to cause a smile to grace your lips."

Amusement struck her. "How would knowing my name help you in attaining your goal of compelling me to smile? Do you suppose that by saying my name in a humorous manner that shall provoke me to laugh?"

His grin widened. "See? You have me again." He crossed his arms. "But we have already shared a close encounter with death, hence I fail to see how anyone might fault us on forgoing with the usual formalities."

He paused.

However when she hesitated he continued, "But of course if you refuse to tell me your name I completely understand. I apologize for my imprudence. Nevertheless, that leaves me with only one other choice." He rubbed his chin in mock consideration as he eyed her. "I shall just have to concoct a nickname for you."

"Please don't put yourself through all that effort." She found herself fighting the urge to smile, because against her better judgment this man charmed her. "My friends already have a nickname for me that you may use. After all, as you said, we aren't truly strangers now are we?" In a playful manner the man threw his head from side to side. "You were my hero yesterday. Hence, I do indeed concede that you ought to know that those closest to me refer to me as, Penny."

"Penny," he quietly repeated her nickname, as if her name warranted reverence. "Lovely. Now whenever I see you I shall ask if you could spare me *a penny for your thoughts.*"

She smirked. "If only I had a penny for every time I heard such nonsense."

He chuckled. "Your smile is priceless, Penny, and I do believe I did finally produce a grin, even if 'twas just a wee one."

She shook her head, but her lips spread from ear to ear. "There, a full smile." She laughed. "I hope you're placated though, because, as a result, my cheeks may very well be sore tomorrow."

"I shall pray that is not the case." He bowed his head slowly. "But I cannot deny being immensely appeased. And since you are far more proper than I, and wouldn't defy convention to ask my name, I shall simply tell you. My friends call me, Blair."

She dipped her chin. "The pleasure has been all mine in meeting you, Blair. For without you, I do believe I would not be here for anyone to call me Penny anymore."

"Then that is a travesty I'm glad I've spared the world." He winked, then looked away from her and out into the crowd. *Which is exactly what she ought to be doing,* she chastised herself.

This man may be handsome, heroic, and amiable, but she must focus on finding P.J. "Excuse me," she told him. Apparently, she had been wrong. She could not think properly in his presence. He had proved to be far too much of a distraction.

Unable to argue, Blair nodded his consent and watched her walk away from him—yet again. Although, her name lingered in his mind. *Penny.* Such a sweet name for a woman with such a clever mind. 'Twas as if her name were at odds with her. And if she had not broken off their conversation, he knew he never would have. Her wit enticed him. Could she really be the woman he had waited for his entire life?

"Uncle Blair, who were you speaking with?" his seven year old niece asked, after she ran to him and jumped into his arms. "She's pretty and has the exact appearance of a princess."

He thoroughly agreed. "She's new in town." He grinned at Elsie.

"Does she practice embroidery?"

"I don't—"

"Will you marry her?"

"I beg your pardon but I believe you're brimming with questions and soon to burst if we don't release them." He tickled his niece.

The wee lass squealed and he relented his attack. "You haven't answered my questions." She eyed him seriously. "Everyone speaks of the fact that you need a wife, Uncle Blair."

"They do, do they?"

She nodded emphatically. "I've heard mention that you work too much. And some of my friends at school said that their mothers said I ought to have a mama. They're certain 'tis not advantageous for me to be raised without one."

He hugged her to him. If only the embrace would cease his heart from rupturing. He loathed that she had to live without a mother. But to endure such talk made the situation even worse. "There are plenty of wonderful women in our family to which you're close to. And I believe we're doing fine, are we not? I'm not so bad, am I?"

"Oh, nay, Uncle Blair. I love you." Her wee arms hugged his neck. "But they are correct that you're not proficient at needlework." He laughed and wrapped his *rough hands*—as Penny had just referred to them—around his niece tighter.

"True." His large hands may be of good use on his farm, but they weren't built for embroidery. He caught a glance of Penny's back as she moved even farther away from him. Penny had long, slender fingers, splendidly fashioned for such fine detailed needlework.

"Uncle Blair, I see Michelle. May I play with her?"

"Of course." He kissed her head then let her drop to her feet. "I shall walk you to her." She smiled and gripped his hand as she pulled him along. "I shall find you when we must leave."

"Thanks, Uncle Blair." She ran to her friend. And he stood and watched her—until his attention was drawn to the woman who twirled the prettiest parasol. How would having Penny on his arm feel? He exhaled sharply as he noted the overly eager greetings she received from more than one eligible bachelor. He was evidently not the only one admiring her.

* * *

"Please excuse us," Pastor West told a small group of people. "I still have many others I must introduce to this young lady." With that, he took Penny's arm and they turned, which put them directly in front of Blair. "Fine day, is it not?"

"It certainly is, Pastor West." Blair dipped his chin as his eyes held Penny's. "And this day continues to better itself."

"Hello, once more." She smiled with enough exaggeration to remind him of their secret joke. To share such covert amusement with this beautiful woman produced an enormous grin on his face, as well.

"Hello again, to you." He bowed. "I see I find myself privileged to be in your presence once more."

"Are you two acquainted?" Pastor West asked.

"Yesterday, Blair saved my life." Her blue eyes danced between him and the pastor.

"Is that so?" The Pastor took his hand and shook it. "Thank you, and God bless you."

He shrugged. "I just behaved as any other man would have."

"Don't be too hasty in assuming that. What you did was unselfish and deserving of praise. You have a true Christian spirit."

He nodded his head reluctantly in thanks. "If I must accept the praise, then you must admit that my actions are a direct result of your counsel. You set a fine example for this community to live by."

"Thank you for saying as much." A wistful expression floated over the pastor's face before he hid his emotions under a smile. Blair was certain his thoughts must have hit upon his recent trouble with his daughter. "I believe no introductions are necessary between the two of you then." Pastor West crossed his arms over his chest.

"On the contrary, Penny and I are lacking in a formal introduction. I have yet to learn her surname."

He met her gaze. Could she perceive the extent to which he wished to be more intimately acquainted with her? There was simply something about her that drew him to her. He leaned back on his heels. *God, is Penny the one for me?*

"Then, we must remedy that posthaste." The pastor smiled. "This is Miss Penelope Sherwood. She's staying with me whilst my daughter, Jamilyn, is away. And Penny, this is Blair McAllister, the most overworked man in town."

He laughed. "Is that how I'm known?"

"Aye, and rightly so. But don't fret. I'm well on my way to finding you a suitable nanny to care for your niece. That should ease your burden some."

"Thank you, I expect it shall."
He took a deep breath. With all the
troublesome dreams Elsie had succumbed
to lately, he hadn't acquired anywhere
close to what was considered adequate
sleep, and that made doing his job
dangerous.

"You have a niece that resides
with you?" Penelope asked.

"Aye." He pointed her out.
"Elsie's seven."

"She's adorable." She watched the
wee lass flounce about in a sweet,
pink gown, before she glanced back at
him. What an admirable man. She didn't
know many men who would take on the
care of a child by themselves. Most
children like Elsie would be sent off
to boarding school, or worse, an
orphan asylum, just as she had been.
"How long has she lived with you?"

"Several months." His eyes
remained on his niece. "Her parents
were in a terrible accident."

Her eyes met his. "I'm sorry." He
dipped his chin and her heart ached to
do something to help this family that
had lost their loved ones. She'd just

lost her pa two months ago and her heart was still shattered. "Pastor West, I must confess that without your knowledge I made plans with your cook earlier today. To thank you for having me to stay I provided your cook with everything she needs to set out a grand feast for you. But with your permission I should also like to invite Blair and Elsie to dine with us?"

"Penny, that wasn't necessary. You needn't repay me." The pastor patted her hand. "But, I thank you, I do appreciate it. And issuing an invitation to Blair and Elsie is an excellent idea."

She turned her smile upon Blair. "Do you have plans for supper?"

"Not besides the usual Sunday suppers I cook when my staff enjoy their day away from work. However, I must confess to using the term *cook* loosely." He smirked.

"Splendid." She clasped her hands together, but laughed when he arched a brow. "'Tis not splendid that you fail to impress with your cooking skills. 'Tis splendid that an excuse to refuse our invitation is nonexistent. And I would like very much to thank you properly for saving my life."

"I don't see how I can refuse now." He dipped his chin. "Not that I would ever have wished to." He grinned. "Thank you for the invitation."

"Wonderful." Pastor West nodded at him. "Then we shall happily await your company." He turned to face her, which forced her to rip her eyes from Blair. "We must continue your introductions."

"Of course." She took his arm and pasted on a smile. She could have remained to speak with Blair the entire afternoon, but that would not help her find P.J. She would just have to wait until this evening to enjoy the pleasure of his company again—at a time when she couldn't be out in search of P.J.

"Good day, Blair," she said, then admired the way he tipped his hat with such elegance. She squeezed her fingers around her parasol and forced herself to look away and set her mind to thoughts of P.J.

How long would her search for P.J. take? If he was in this town he ought to be at church. She tried to think of reasons for his absence, such as him being ill. But 'twas July, and illness was a rarity in the summer months.

She shuddered. She didn't want to entertain any thoughts that something bad may have happened to him that physically prevent him from attending church. And she surely didn't wish to conclude that whoever held him captive would ignore his spiritual needs. But then, where was he?

"Pastor West." A woman waved as she bustled toward them. "You must accompany me back to the church. This heat has warped several windows and I cannot close them."

He turned a smile on her. "I shall be but a moment."

"Don't rush on my account." She withdrew her arm from his and strolled through the crowd. P.J. had to be among the parishioners somewhere.

"Fine looking day." A gigantic form blocked her path. She craned her neck to look up at the towering man.

His eyes roamed over her, which made her stomach ill. She wasn't cattle that needed to be appraised for auction.

With her arms crossed she stepped back. "Aye, 'tis a nice day. And if you'll excuse me, I wish to continue my walk."

"Allow me accompany you." The man stepped closer to her. "Since you're alone you must be in need of a man."

She opened her mouth to decline his offer, but before she could, Blair's voice came deep and strong from behind her. "Clyde."

Relief filled her. She wasn't sure this burly man would have taken her refusal well.

"Blair." Clyde pinned his chin to his chest. "I was just about to join this beautiful woman on a walk." He winked at her, and Blair's eyes hit her with a stunned expression.

Her mouth gaped. She had not one moment's thought toward going anywhere with this man.

He must have seen her disapproval because his jaw unclenched. "Sorry, Clyde. 'Tis past time we depart," he spoke firmly and her eyebrows pinched together. Were Blair and this man friends? Nay, they couldn't be. She couldn't fathom them having any similarities or common interests.

"Clyde, where's Paul?" Blair's words struck her like blows to the chest. Her head darted about in search of Paul. Surely Blair couldn't be referring to Paul Jonah, her P.J.? There must be another Paul in this town. But still her heart stopped as she searched for him.

"He's over yonder." Clyde pointed. "The dandy wished to examine something more closely. Whatever he fancies though, I haven't the faintest."

Blair appeared to be only half-listening to Clyde as he called out, "Paul!" Uncontrollably, she stepped forward beside Blair to garner a better vantage point.

However, when she nearly bumped into him she didn't return his glance or excuse her behavior. Her eyes were focused on the spot Clyde had pointed to. She had to see Paul for herself.

God, please, please, let him be my P.J.

The anticipation of waiting for Paul to turn around made her chest hurt. How long could she hold her breath or allow her heart to beat with such a volatile rhythm before she suffered some sort of malady? *Please, God, please*, she repeated.

With a sharp intake of breath she saw him. The man she'd been searching for. Her brother was alive. But from this distance she couldn't ascertain if he had suffered any abuse. However, he was able to walk and that made a smile burn forth from her heart.

She would have run to him but she caught Blair staring at her. Realizing how bizarre she must appear, standing there, grinning affectionately, whilst Clyde merely looked at the man, she whacked her fan open and covered her face. She couldn't permit anyone to have even the slightest inkling that she knew Paul. But Blair continued to stare at her and curiosity fought for understanding in his eyes.

"Coming," Paul shouted as he ambled toward them.

Now she understood exactly why
Blair had told her that his job
involved watching people. Clyde must
be a prisoner of war, along with P.J.,
and Blair was their warden.

She fanned herself. She needed
the extra air. She never imagined that
she'd meet P.J. with people about her.
Somehow she thought she would find him
alone, or at least be able to talk
with him privately beforehand. P.J.
wasn't expecting her and he might do
an even worse job than she had at
hiding his surprise to see her. If
only she could impart a signal to him
somehow. But how would she accomplish
that?

Scared at revealing their
relationship, she fumbled backward.
She couldn't allow P.J. to see her. If
people realized they knew each other
severe trouble would certainly follow.
Someone might think she had come here
to help him escape. And that would
lead to terrible suffering for both of
them.

"Excuse me. I must assist Pastor
West's cook with supper," she rushed

her words out from under her fan as
P.J. approached.

Blair's keen eyes remained on
her, and she couldn't help but fidget
with her fan. "Until to-night then."
She gave a nod, then jerked her body
around and hustled away, still unable
to grasp that Blair was P.J.'s warden.

She should be relieved. Blair
didn't seem akin to the sort of man
who would hurt someone. Although, he
had pushed her rather indelicately
yesterday. And after he'd rescued her,
she had seen him fight with that man
in front of the general store.
Moreover, he certainly had enough
muscle under his command.

Nay. She shook her head. He
couldn't be a violent man. He had
pushed her to save her life. And he
had looked with such love at his
niece. Surely a man with that much
love in his eyes wouldn't harm others.

She rounded the corner of the
church then stopped to peer back. She
knew that just because a man was good
to his niece did not count as evidence
that he wasn't a harsh warden to his
prisoners. They were, after all,

British, and in this war that made them enemies.

Nevertheless, whatever kind of man Blair was, she would ascertain his exact character once and for all. She had come here to ensure P.J. was well and she wouldn't leave until she had. If Blair abused his prisoners she would cause an uproar and put an end to it. She wouldn't leave P.J. here to suffer.

If only she could speak with P.J. alone. But how? Should she wait until church next week? Nay, that was too long. Anything could happen to him in a week. She inhaled a deep breath. She knew exactly what she must do.

She trudged home as the plan took form in her mind. When Blair came to dine with them for supper she somehow needed to convince him to employ her as Elsie's nanny.

Blair assisted Elsie down from their wagon. "Your hand, m'lady?"

She giggled, then reached up and tucked her wee fingers into the crook of his arm. "Look, Uncle Blair." Her eyes widened as they neared Pastor West's home. "There's that princess from earlier."

He laughed and waved to the radiant woman who stood amidst a field of wildflowers. "Miss Penelope Sherwood, may I introduce you to Miss Elsie Williamson."

"Pleased to make your acquaintance." Penny curtseyed. "I was picking some flowers for the supper table, would you care to help me?"

"Aye, please." Elsie grinned. "I adore flowers."

"Fabulous. Then that's one thing we have in common."

Elsie stopped to look up at Penny, a serious expression creased her small features. "Do you also enjoy eating peaches and doing embroidery?"

"I do. I'm looking forward to next month when the peaches ripen on the trees." Penny bent down to talk with Blair's niece. "And after supper, if you wish, I could show you my latest piece of embroidery?"

"Oh, please do." Elsie smiled then turned to him. "I shall be most pleased if you marry her." She skipped off.

His jaw went slack. Penny's blue eyes stared at him. His cravat strangled him. "I'm sorry, did I miss something?" she chuckled.

He nodded and closed his eyelids slowly before he opened them in the same tortured manner. "It seems some well-meaning folks have been telling Elsie I ought to marry."

"Ah." She dipped her chin as a smirk graced her lips. "So she didn't procure the idea from you?"

"Me?" His hand hit his chest. "Nay." He shook his head but stopped when her eyebrows shot up. "Sorry, I didn't intend for my emphatic *nay* to imply that you wouldn't make a fine wife, 'tis just that I wouldn't put such fanciful ideas in Elsie's head."

She laughed. "You need not explain. I understand. I was merely jesting." He wiped his forehead with the back of his hand. The noose around his neck loosened. This July heat was unbearable. "After all, Mr. McAllister, we were only properly introduced earlier today."

Her use of his family name made him grin. "True. But do you not believe in love at first sight, Miss Sherwood?" He held her gaze, and if she guessed his feelings toward her he shan't deny them.

She flustered with hesitation. "If you posed that question to the lasses I attended school with they would cry with laughter, because they always teased me for having extensive romantic notions."

He sucked in a breath. Had she felt the same instantaneous connection he had after they had first met.

"Are these enough flowers?" Elsie held forth a bouquet larger than her head.

"Aye, and I particularly adore the daisies you picked." Penny took the flowers to admire them more closely. "However, if you wish to pick more there's also an empty vase in the parlor."

"Oh, 'twould be my pleasure." His niece bounded back into the sea of color.

"She's a sweet lass."

"Aye." He watched Elsie. "But she suffers much. I know she misses her life before she came to live with me."

"You must be suffering, as well."

He nodded. But didn't elaborate. He didn't know if she actually wished to hear about his woes or if she were merely being polite. Did she want to know about Elsie's troublesome dreams and the secrets that had nearly torn his family apart?

"Ah!" Elsie cried.

With Penny by his side they ran to her. "What has happened?" He embraced his niece.

"It hurts," she muttered between sobs.

Penny smoothed her slender fingers through the lass' brown hair. "Where is the pain?" she cooed.

"My arm." Elsie held her wee arm up.

Penny examined the appendage. "You've been stung by a bee." She pulled out the stinger.

"Ah!" Elsie wailed once more. He held his niece tighter.

"I'm sorry." Penny patted her hair. "Come to the well and apply cool water."

"Will that stop my arm from hurting." Red eyes looked upon her arm with disdain.

"When I'm hurt the water always soothes me." Penny shot him a pained expression. He carried Elsie to the well. He knew, just as Penny must, that this sting would likely hurt for several hours despite any remedy they applied.

"Here." Penny soaked her handkerchief, then held the cloth over the red spot on his niece's arm. "Better?"

Elsie nodded.

"Do you wish to take this water inside and continue to cool your sore?" she asked. Elsie nodded. The amusement of playing with water tipped her lips up. "Then we shall secure a special place for your water bowl at the table," she assured her. Elsie giggled and Blair asked God once more if He had sent Penny to him.

"I must apologize profusely, Blair," Penelope whispered as they ambled to Pastor West's house. Her eyes remained on Elsie, who walked a few steps ahead of them, completely engrossed with dabbing at her sting. How would she ever convince him to permit her be Elsie's nanny when 'twas her fault his niece was now injured?

"You needn't apologize. I've been stung more times than I can count. And besides, Elsie's my responsibility, if there was any blame to be laid, that blame would be entirely mine to bear."

She wrung her hands. She didn't know how to proceed. This was not at all how she foresaw this evening unfolding.

"Actually, Penny, I think 'tis I who now needs to offer you my gratitude."

Her head shot toward him. "Whatever for?"

"For tending Elsie with such swiftness and compassion."

She forced herself to swallow. This was her chance. "Then I must insist you do as I did, Blair, and don't actually say the words *thank you.*" She met his eyes as his lips twitched upward at her crafty comment and a grin spread across her own lips. "Instead, I wish you to grant me a request."

He chuckled as his eyebrows pinched together. "You've excited my curiosity yet again. What possible request could I grant you? And why are we to have such a hard time thanking each other?"

She laughed. "I suppose 'tis a conundrum between us. And yet my request would give us far more opportunity to work on that particular facet of etiquette, if you wish to rectify it."

"Please tell me how." His brown eyes held merriment, which sent her heart ricocheting around in her chest.

"I was hoping you would consider employing me as Elsie's nanny," she rushed her words out before she lost her nerve. Then she stared at Blair not even daring to breathe.

"Elsie's nanny?" His eyes narrowed.

"Aye. I do believe Pastor West said he hoped to find someone."

"Did I just hear my name?" Pastor West's cheerful voice came from behind.

"Aye." Her head swung around to greet him.

"Good, then we have our first topic of conversation for supper already chosen." He grinned. "And that is precisely why I'm out of doors—supper is ready." He strode past them to open the door, however his smile faded when he beheld Elsie. "Were you hurt?"

"I was stung by the most vicious bee." Elsie held up her arm for the pastor to examine, and Penelope told him about the bowl of water she'd promised to keep beside her.

"I see." Pastor West stepped into the house. "I think that's a fine remedy." He called for his cook, then took the bucket from Blair and relayed the instructions to the woman.

"Ye come with me, Elsie." The pastor's cook cuddled Elsie into her side. "Little girls who've suffered bee stings deserve a taste of dessert before supper." Elsie squealed with pleasure, and the adults laughed as they sat at the table on the opposite side of the kitchen.

"*Thank you*, Blair," Penelope emphasized her gratitude when he held out a chair for her. "See, proper etiquette just requires practice." He nodded his head with amusement.

"I believe I've missed something." The pastor seated himself. "Are you both in need of practicing your manners?"

She flushed. "Actually, Pastor West, I was alluding to the conversation Blair and I were speaking of before you came upon us. You heard your name because I was speaking to Blair about the nanny you are helping him ascertain for Elsie."

"A nanny?" Elsie's red eyes glared at Blair. "Do you not wish to care for me any longer?"

Blair rushed to the child, and Penelope bit her lip. She'd distressed the child again. How many times would she be the cause of this little lass' tears? This was definitely not the correct approach needed to convince Blair she could be a decent nanny.

"Of course I still wish to care for you." Blair squeezed her little shoulders as he bent down on one knee. "But you must understand that I don't possess the time to care for you in the manner that you ought to be cared for."

"But a nanny shan't care for me, Uncle Blair. Back home, my friend had a nanny, and her nanny pinched her every time she was displeased with her—which was exceedingly often. I'm not fond of pain. Pinching hurts, just as much as this sting, and I know for a fact such torment leaves bruises."

He stroked Elsie's arms. "I'm aggrieved for your friend, but I promise not to hire anyone who shall pinch you."

"You cannot promise that, because once the nanny arrives your presence shall diminish and then you shan't even be aware of how I'm treated. My friend never saw her parents."

"I shan't disappear," he tried to console her, and Penelope's heart ached for them. The poor child had enough to contend with after the loss of her parents, she didn't need to fret about the possibility of being injured by a nanny.

"Promise?" Elsie's eyes welled and Penelope's nearly did, as well.

"Aye. I shan't allow anyone to hurt you." He kissed her forehead. "And Pastor West is helping me find a good, kind nanny. We shan't settle for anyone less than ideal." Elsie peered at the pastor and he nodded. "Now, how about we enjoy our supper." Blair rose and guided Elsie to her chair. "Please don't be distressed. I shan't hire a nanny without your approval."

"Truly?" Elsie sat and looked up pleadingly at him.

"I promise I shan't." He pushed her chair in, then dropped into the one beside it.

Penelope smiled. He'd exhausted himself to calm his niece, and that made his effort even more endearing. Unfortunately for her though, the subject was now closed, and she didn't know when she would be able to procure another chance to broach the conversation. She wouldn't risk having Elsie overhear her a second time. She would never knowingly upset that sweet, little lass, and hopefully, Blair knew as much.

She took up her glass and shook her hand slightly. The liquid swirled around just below the rim before she took a sip. She did sincerely wish to be Elsie's nanny now for more than just P.J.'s sake. She firmly believed she could benefit Elsie—even despite the terrible mishaps of this day—because she knew they had far more in common than a mere love for flowers, peaches, and embroidery. And with God's help, maybe she could use her wretched past to help Elsie's future.

Blair sank into the comfort of Pastor West's parlor sofa, his stomach full of food fit to be served to President James Madison.

"I enjoy summer." The pastor eased into the cushion beside him. "But I do miss the roar of the fire in the hearth on evenings such as this when I'm apt to sit here and enjoy a hot cup of tea."

Blair nodded. Although, that serene image appeared only as a distant fantasy. It had been such a long while since he'd even had a moment to himself, let alone enjoy that aforesaid luxury. And alarmingly, a voice in his head declared his situation changeable if he employed Penny.

His eyes sought her. She sat across from him showing Elsie her embroidery. He never would have imagined that such a woman would offer to be Elsie's nanny. He may not know all the particulars of her life, but he knew from the material of her clothes that she came from a wealthy family. And she carried herself with an enormous amount of grace. Even now, as they all sat resting, she sat properly with her feet crossed at the ankles and her back never touching the chair.

So what had compelled her to pursue work as Elsie's nanny? Dare he hope she wished to be near him? Or that she might harbor affection for the child? Nay. She could simply satisfy herself on those accounts by meeting with them socially.

Somehow, despite how she dressed, she must be in need of money. Perhaps she was estranged from her family, or she wished an income in which to begin life anew for herself here.

Or was there another reason? He mused as he beheld her. That is, until she glanced up and caught him staring at her. With a cough he turned to peer into the empty hearth. Thankfully there hadn't been a fire this night because he already found the air fairly warm in this small room.

"Uncle Blair?" Elsie said his name as a question.

"Aye." He turned his head unable to resist meeting Penny's beautiful blue eyes.

"May I invite the princess to visit us to-morrow for a tea party? I wish for her to see my embroidery."

"The princess?" Penny looked between him and Elsie.

He smirked at Elsie's answer, "I refer to you as the princess, because of your beauty, and you don the loveliest clothes I've ever seen, just as I suppose a princess would."

"You are a darling lass." Penny ran a hand over Elsie's cheek.

"So, Uncle Blair?" Elsie insisted. "Is she permitted to attend my tea party?"

He raked unsteady fingers through his hair. This was not the proper style in which to invite a lady to their home. Penny would feel compelled to accept Elsie's invitation and he would never wish her to visit under duress.

"Elsie, your uncle's rather busy," she interjected, and a knot formed in his stomach. He'd been correct. She wished to put forth an excuse so as not to upset his niece. "But perhaps I may visit some other day."

His eyebrow hitched. He'd been mistaken. "I may be unrelentingly busy, Penny, but I would surely welcome your visit. And to-morrow is just fine." The bluest eyes met his and he felt the magnitude of her gaze before she looked down at her embroidery.

"Oh, goody." Elsie bounced up and down.

"Pastor West, you're more than welcome to join in, as well," he extended the invitation.

"I'm afraid I've committed myself elsewhere to-morrow." The pastor took up his teacup. "I must see to several of my parishioners."

"Of course." Blair dipped his chin. "Another time perhaps?"

"Most definitely." The pastor sipped his tea.

"Elsie, the hour grows late." He sat forward on the sofa.

"Must we leave already?" she groaned.

"Aye," Penny added. "Must you retire this early?"

He cleared his throat. He hadn't expected Penny to protest his retreat. Was he a fool to hope she might harbor feelings for him as he did for her?

"I apologize, but I'm afraid we must." He pushed his hands down the length of his trousers. "Tending to my prisoners once more this evening is a necessity."

"Prisoners of war?" Penelope's breath caught in her lungs. She had to monopolize on this opportunity to unearth any information she could regarding P.J. and the treatment he faced. She'd despaired over how to broach the subject the entire night, but failed to devise a way that wouldn't expose her as overly interested. And her fear of being discovered as P.J.'s sister had roiled her stomach with such frequency she was surprised she even ate supper.

"Aye, Penny." Pastor West rested his teacup on a side table. "Blair is a warden for British prisoners of war." She nodded. She couldn't very well utter anything to reveal she already possessed that knowledge.

"Considering you're British, I hope my profession doesn't upset you?" His brown eyes delved into hers.

She bit her lip, then shook her head. "I understand these situations are a necessity in times of war." She glanced at Elsie, the lass' sweet, innocent face tilted up. She smiled at her. This was not the time to inquire whether Blair tortured his prisoners. "I just hope my presence doesn't upset anyone in town."

"I cannot fathom why anyone would be upset." Pastor West threw his hands up.

Blair nodded. "'Tis not as if you harbor an intention to interfere in this war."

She swallowed hard. If either of them knew her true reason for being here they wouldn't speak this pleasantly to her, because as the sister of one of those prisoners of war she would never be viewed as a harmless onlooker. And she would send herself and P.J. straight into the depths of danger if she ever forgot that and let her feelings for Blair or Elsie cloud that truth.

Nevertheless, she wasn't about to back down in the face of peril. To-morrow, she would use Blair and Elsie's invitation as an occasion to explore Blair's property. And God willing, she would locate P.J. before anyone found her, because if Blair didn't employ her as Elsie's nanny she might not obtain another opportunity to investigate his land.

*O*n the edge of the
forest surrounding
Blair's property,
Penelope peered out
from behind a maple
tree's wide trunk. His
home appeared welcoming, but she
couldn't admire Elsie's needlework, or

enjoy a cup of tea, just yet. She must first search Blair's homestead to locate P.J.

Please, God, help me find him quickly. The summer's morning air entangled itself around her ankles as she lifted her skirts to hurry on.

Creeping through the shadows, she ran from tree to tree, furtively looking over her shoulder and thanking God that not a soul caught sight of her.

But without a map of Blair's land or knowledge of anyone's routines, she was in danger of stumbling upon someone at every turn. And if that happened, how would she explain lurking about his land?

She shook her head. She mustn't fret. She wouldn't cower. She needed to press on. However, she paused when her foot cracked a branch and a swift warm breeze erupted out of the forest. Her hair was blown away from her ears and 'twas as if God Himself whispered to her, *keep going.*

She rushed on, until she heard a voice echo through the woods. With her body hugged to a tree's trunk, she stood motionless, even though her body itched to increase the distance between herself and a large, black bug that crawled up the tree next to her head.

Disgusting! She pursed her lips and focused on the voice. She couldn't decipher any of the words, but the speaker was definitely female and seemed to be speaking to herself.

As the voice grew fainter, she sprang away from the hideous insect and quickly hid behind another tree. Peeking around that tree, she spotted the speaker and recognized her immediately. She'd met her at church yesterday. 'Twas Blair's cook, Halcyon. And to her relief, the woman had her back to her as she followed a path Penelope assumed led to Blair's house.

But where had Blair's cook come from? Her gaze darted about. There didn't appear to be anything this far from the house. However, there had to be a reason why she'd journeyed this far.

She trudged on, determined to discover where that woman had been, because if Halcyon had brought the prisoners of war their breakfast, then she might finally locate P.J.

Then again—she stopped—perhaps Blair's cook ventured this far for another reason? Perhaps Blair was nearby and she'd brought him something. Her chest constricted. She must be mindful to keep herself completely hidden.

Once more she prayed as she crept slowly forward.

But, the sight of a small log cabin ceased her movement. Could that be P.J.'s enclosure? Hope filled her. She looked in every possible direction, searching for even a hint of anyone who might catch her.

The forest was completely devoid of human sounds—besides her own heart thumping hard against her chest. But she wouldn't wither in fear. She'd hazarded this much. She needed to see whether P.J. was in that cabin.

She tiptoed closer, careful not to emit a sound. The door was closed. She rounded the corner, and slunk along a wall until she could crouch under a window. She prayed that if

P.J. spied her, she wouldn't give him a fright.

With the slowness of a snail, she lifted her head to peer into the dwelling.

She gasped.

With her hand clamped over her mouth, she fell to her knees. Her head ached with questions at what she'd seen. Why was Blair housing such a woman on his land? Was she a prisoner of war?

A shiver ripped through her, an eerie feeling of foreboding, as if she'd just encountered her future self.

Then realization struck. What if this woman wasn't a prisoner? She could very well venture forth and discover her prowling.

Making haste, she crawled away from the cabin, then ran to distance herself from the woman in the woods.

Out of breath, she leaned a hand against a tree, pinched her side and winced as the air stung her lungs. The sooner she located her brother and fulfilled their pa's dying wish, the quicker she could return to Upper

Canada and leave all this dangerous espionage behind.

And yet, that woman's image reverberated inside her mind—brown hair, neatly pulled back away from her face and tied at the nape of her neck. She was clothed entirely in black, as she sat deathly still in a wooden rocking chair, and stared down at her lap. If she had been elderly, Penelope would have assumed she was infirm, but the woman didn't appear much older than she. And despite her frown lines, she was pretty.

Penelope rubbed her eyes. She had to vanquish these thoughts until she returned to the safety of Pastor West's home. She still needed to find P.J.

The faint sound of whistling weaved through the forest. She willed her feet to move over the fallen pine needles. She desperately needed to vacate the woods and locate the path she'd followed from Pastor West's house.

With hands fisted into her skirts she ran. A bird fluttered from a tree branch overhead. Her heart soared with trepidation. Then, with a jerk, she was halted. Her dress had caught in some thorns. "Not now," she muttered, her fingers fumbled to free the material.

Perspiration threatened to sting her eyes. 'Twas hopeless. She must rip the material to set herself free. She growled at the thorns. Then took a firm hold of the silk. On *the count of three. One, two*—

"Penny?"

She jumped. Her gown tore.

"Why are wandering these parts?"

Her breath caught in her throat. But 'twas just as well, because not one plausible explanation sprung to mind. "Blair—I—um—"

"Your dress is torn."

"Aye." She fondled the material—anything to avoid his piercing gaze. "'Twas caught in thorns."

"Are you fine otherwise?"

She nodded against the weight of his curiosity. "I was en route to visit with you and Elsie."

"Did you walk the entire distance from Pastor West's?"

She nodded again. "He had need of his wagon."

"Did he not give you instructions as to the precise location of my house, because you're a good distance from it?" She dared a glance at him. His eyebrows were pinched together with either concern or confusion. She squeezed her hands together in hope that he wasn't suspicious of her behavior. He shook his head. "It matters not. But, if I had known, I would have come to collect you, or your visit could have been postponed for another day."

She fidgeted with the frayed edges around the rip in her dress. "I've always enjoyed a fine walk, and besides, I wouldn't wish to disappoint Elsie. She was rather earnest in her invitation."

"That she was—is." He smiled and her pulse slowed its erratic beat. He must have assumed her lost, because he didn't question her further. "Elsie was determined to prepare a special tea party for you. She enlisted our cook to manage every minute detail."

"She's such a sweet lass." She let her skirt drop.

"'Twas sweet of you to accept her offer." His eyes held hers.

She forgot to breathe. Then, she smiled briefly, before she diverted her gaze. She did indeed wish to be in Elsie's company. His, as well. But she was here for her brother and now her chance had vanished. "If you would be so kind as to direct me to your home, I ought to hurry, I shan't wish to keep Elsie waiting any longer."

He dipped his chin. "If you'll permit me, I shall convey you there myself."

"Are you afraid I may lose my way?" she teased. Although, she did wonder if perhaps he was concerned about her happening upon something he didn't wish her to see—such as the woman in that cabin?

He rubbed the back of his neck. A mischievous grin crept onto his lips. "Your absence would be sorely felt."

Her heart raced. If only he wasn't her brother's warden. She dipped her head to the side, and watched her hand sweep along a bush that prickled her fingers.

Pulling her arm back, she clasped her hands together. Her hope was in vain. He was her brother's warden. That couldn't be altered. And besides, even though he was handsome and charming, she still hadn't ascertained his character as a warden. Although, God knew she prayed he was benevolent.

"Blair." She glanced up at him. "May I inquire as to whether you've considered my request to become Elsie's nanny?"

She held her breath as she waited for his response. If he denied her, she'd be forced to attempt to speak with her brother at church. And that opportunity only presented itself once a week. Moreover, with that many people about, she doubted she'd be able to maneuver them into a tête-à-tête, and a private conversation was the only way in which she would tell her brother that their pa had died.

"I have," he said. However, he didn't elaborate. His eyes met hers, but his facial expression didn't reveal a single hint as to whether he favored the idea or not.

She squeezed her hands together even firmer. His silence grew her distress. She fought to remain composed. But she couldn't refrain from speech much longer. He hadn't spoken for several minutes. Although if her feelings told time they'd insist hours had passed. "And?"

"And—we've arrived," he raised his voice, as if to announce their presence. Then he swung his arm out ahead of him and gestured for her to enter the pathway that led up to his two-storey home.

"You've come," Elsie's voice sailed out his front door, as she rushed down the pathway to meet them. Her long brown hair waved in welcome. "I've been unable to sit still the entire day." She beamed. "I just cannot fathom that I'm to host a princess at my tea party," she squealed. Penelope couldn't stifle her laughter. Elsie had a knack for making her forget her troubles.

She took the little lass' outstretched hand. "I'm delighted to attend your party." She let Elsie lead her into the drawing room. "Everything is fashioned beautifully." She walked to the neatly arranged table. "You truly are expecting royalty."

Elsie giggled at her compliment. She smiled at her, then glanced at Blair, impressed that he had allowed Elsie the use of such a fine tea set. Penelope had never been allowed to touch anything of such high quality until she was an adult.

The silver was lovely, and the fine bone China cups and saucers were extremely fancy. There was even a plate stacked with biscuits, and a delicate vase with pretty flowers. Surely Elsie had exerted a good deal of effort into this tea.

"Thank you for inviting me." She looked from Elsie to Blair, who pulled a chair back for her. She grinned up at him as she sat. *"Thank you."*

"Thank you for obliging us," he responded, omitting any doubt in her mind that he also welcomed the chance to tease her with a joke only the two of them understood.

"I simply love being seven years old." Elsie held the plate of biscuits out to her. "When I was six, I wasn't permitted to drink tea. But after I turned seven my parents finally conceded." Her smile faded.

She must miss her parents dreadfully. "I've always been fond of the number seven." Penelope took a biscuit, then passed the plate to Blair, who had seated himself on her left. "When I was seven, I dreamed of having seven of everything." She attempted to buoy the lass' spirits. "Seven bunnies, seven dolls, seven brothers, seven sisters—"

A spark lit Elsie's eyes once more. "Seven of everything?" She giggled, as Blair poured their tea. "Even seven mothers and seven fathers?"

Penelope sighed. "Fourteen hugs and kisses goodnight."

"But fourteen people telling you what you ought to do and what you ought not to do." Elsie laughed. "I have Uncle Blair and he's enough."

"Ahem." Blair made a mournful face at Elsie. When the lass shook her head, evidently not believing his pretense, he laughed.

"Perhaps you're correct, Elsie." Penelope shot him an amused look. "I would have been more than content with one mother and one father."

"Did you not have parents?" Elsie asked. Penelope blinked several times, unable to comprehend why she had divulged such intimate information, now she would need to explain. Her eyes held Blair's briefly, an intense interest awaited her answer.

"Everyone has parents." She turned to face Elsie, and after a deep breath she continued, "But I wasn't fortunate enough to meet my true parents until I was an adolescent and they adopted my brother and myself."

"You were adopted?" Elsie's jaw dropped.

"Elsie," Blair corrected her as he set the nearly empty teapot down.

"Nay, 'tis fine." She touched his arm. Then jerked her hand away. She should never have offered such an intimate gesture. "She's merely curious." Her lip curled at the lass. "Aye, I was adopted, Elsie."

"Then your parents passed away just as mine have?" Penelope was certain she heard something snap in Blair's chest and break his heart. The anguish in his eyes was immense. She grimaced. He must grieve every minute of every day attempting to ease his niece's pain. "My parents perished in a boat accident."

"I'm sorry for your loss." She stroked Elsie's hair. "My parents weren't deceased though." Elsie's shoulders slumped, as if she had longed to share her pain with someone and Penelope had disappointed her. "They may have perished by now, though," she uttered. "They abandoned my brother and I when we were infants. We never saw or heard from them ever again."

"That's terrible." Elsie touched her arm. The act of someone that young offering her comfort dismayed her, just as she knew the sentiment must torment Blair. "I understand. Being abandoned hurts."

He opened his mouth to protest, but she spoke first, "Your parents didn't choose to abandon you." She gently pushed a lock of his niece's fine hair off her cheek. "God called them home."

Tears welled in her languished eyes. "Then I hate God." She pulled away from Penelope.

But she reached out for her again. "You mustn't say or entertain such thoughts."

Elsie clanked her teacup into its saucer. "Why ever not?"

"Because God has a reason for all He does, even if we don't understand."

"Penny's correct." The compassion in Blair's eyes hit her. And she knew—more than ever—how much she wished to become Elsie's nanny. She had to help this little lass. Penelope knew desolation. She knew loss and heartache. And perhaps through her, God could heal Elsie.

"It's all very disagreeable." Elsie's bottom lip trembled.

"Aye, life can offer much sorrow," she agreed. "But there are always blessings. You must always seek out the blessings. For instance, you have your uncle."

"He's perpetually busy. I must play alone much of the time." She peered down into her lap. "I wish my mama still lived."

Blair's jaw clenched. "I do try." He reached out and held his niece's hand. "Whenever I manage a spare moment I do allot my time to you." He rubbed his thumb over her skin. "Such as now. But I must work, as well." His tone was soothing, but she was sure guilt ate at his insides. "Just as you do, I wish things had come to pass differently."

"So I wouldn't be living here with you?" A tear escaped Elsie's eye.

"Nay!" He lifted her chin. "I love you."

"But I'm a burden," she whimpered. "My friends confided that they overheard their mothers say I shall be the reason you never marry."

"Ridiculous," Penelope exclaimed. "I was adopted, and if someone truly loves your uncle she shall love you, as well. She would be a fool not to. And if she's a fool, I dare say your uncle shall show better sense than to court such an imbecile."

Elsie's lips curled. She peered with hope at her uncle. He nodded emphatically. "Penny is absolutely correct. And if you shall permit me to boast—" he puffed his chest "—I do possess more sense than to marry a foolish woman."

"I'm glad." Elsie giggled, and she joined her. Blair leaned over and kissed the top of his niece's forehead, then pulled her into a hug. He mouthed the words *thank you* over her head.

These unspoken words fell upon her differently. They'd never uttered those words, except to tease one another. She dipped her chin, deeply pleased with the force of his gratitude.

"We have just happened upon a wondrous discovery though." Elsie's little eyes sparkled back to life.

She exchanged a confused look with Blair.

"Please elaborate." He took a mouthful of tea.

"If she lacks knowledge of her parents, then perhaps they were royalty." His niece eyed her. "She may actually be a real princess."

Penelope laughed.

"Perhaps," he agreed and playfully assessed her. "She does exhibit a certain je ne sais quoi."

"Aye," Elsie agreed.

She wished she had her fan opened to hide the blush that had surely crept up her face.

"How fortunate to be a princess," Elsie sighed.

"It pains me to disappoint you, but I doubt I'm a princess," Penelope chuckled.

"But you're exceedingly pretty," Elsie argued. "Far beyond comparison." Her face scrunched up in serious contemplation. "Do you not think so, Uncle Blair?"

The brown in his eyes darkened. "Aye." He didn't waver in his attention to her. "She is, indisputably, an exceptional beauty."

Her heart fluttered uncontrollably. "Thank you," she murmured. The room had shrunk, and she was glad they were seated, because her knees were jelly.

"Alas, there is more to owning the title of a princess than mere appearance," Blair told his niece, without moving his eyes away from her. "She must possess certain admirable qualities."

She neglected her need for air. Did he actually hold her in such high esteem?

"True." Elsie nodded with importance. "Do you possess those fine qualities?" She turned an eager face toward her. Penelope's mouth gaped.

"Elsie," Blair laughed. "Perhaps we've embarrassed our guest."

"I'm sorry," she uttered, her expression one of apprehension.

"You need not apologize," Penelope assured her. "There are far greater atrocities than being compared to a princess."

"I do sincerely hope we haven't offended you. We would never intentionally cause you discomfort. And I trust you shall not refuse to be in our company henceforth?" He arched a brow, and gave his niece a look that Penelope was sure held meaning, even though she couldn't fathom what.

"Oh, nay, I hope not." Panic seized Elsie's small features, as she darted her eyes back and forth between the two adults.

"I assure you that is not the case." Penelope smirked, and shook her head, before she took the last sip of her tea. What had he alluded to?

"Excellent." His smile widened. "Because Elsie wishes to ask something of you."

Penelope hesitated. She stared first at Blair, then at his niece, both of which wore immense grins on their faces.

"Even though you may not be a real princess, I hope you shall permit me to consider you one?" Elsie's face grew serious.

That was the question? Had Blair actually discussed this topic with his niece? She chuckled. "I fail to see how such a belief could be hurtful."

"Perfect, because 'twould be a great honor to have a princess as my nanny."

Her eyes flew to Blair's. "You wish me to be her nanny?" she nearly choked on her words. She had been prepared to assert her merits, prove she could not only handle the work, but excel in the post. She never imagined they would simply offer the station to her.

He nodded. "Pastor West heralds your praises. And I highly value his opinion. When pressed, he had not one negative utterance. Furthermore, as I told Elsie, I truly intended to uphold my promise to seek her consent." He smiled. "She is rather fond of you."

"More than fond." Elsie shook her head at him. "I believe we shall be bosom friends."

"I cannot think of anything that would please me more." Her eyes welled, as she stroked the lass' hair. Her sole purpose was supposed to be her brother, but she couldn't confine her heart to a box. This sweet lass needed her. She just needed to find a solution that benefited everyone.

"This was a lovely tea party." Blair beamed at his niece. "But alas, I must return to work."

"I understand," she said. The weight he carried lessened. She didn't harbor ill feelings toward him. *Thank You, God. You know my greatest wish is to see her happy.* He'd been praying about her daily, and would continue.

"Elsie, would you please help Halcyon clear away the tea?"

"Certainly." Elsie grinned mischievously, "But first, I need one more biscuit."

He chuckled. His smile met Penny's expressive blue eyes. "May I speak with you privately?" he asked. "We could take a turn about the garden."

"Certainly." She folded her napkin and placed the linen on the table, whilst he rose to help her from her seat. "I must thank you once more, Elsie." She stood. "Upon my return, I most definitely do wish to see your embroidery."

Elsie nodded. "Do hurry then."

She laughed as she followed Blair. "Elsie thoroughly enjoyed herself," he said, as he led her out of doors. "I dare say, she may request a daily tea party." He motioned for her to accompany him down a path that led to his garden.

"Then I shall encourage her to do so. The practice shall be beneficial for when she becomes the lady of her own house." He regarded her. There was nary a doubt in his mind that she would be a fabulous nanny. And he had to admit, he would enjoy her presence, as well.

"I must warn you." He interrupted his thoughts. "Elsie suffers from frightening dreams."

"That's understandable." She looked at the dirt underfoot. "For one that young, she's been given more than her fair share to contend with."

"That she has," he agreed. "And due to that—" his body went rigid "—I must dictate one rule, that I must insist you follow implicitly."

"Pray tell?" Penny stopped and glared at him, distress creased her eyes.

*E*ven though a warm breeze passed over Penelope, she still shivered. She didn't appreciate Blair's austere tone, and his steely posture didn't bode well. What rule did he speak of?

And why had he spoken as if 'twere a matter of such dire importance?

"You and Elsie are free to come and go as you please. And I insist you consider my house your home, but—" his eyes darkened "—you are never to set foot past the barn, nor allow Elsie to venture thus far."

"What lays beyond the barn?" the question escaped her lips the moment he ceased his speech.

"As far as Elsie's concerned—the end of the earth."

"Pardon?" Her eyebrows slammed together. "I shan't lie to the lass."

"Of course, but you shall enforce this rule, both for Elsie and yourself." He raked his fingers through his hair. "You must understand the severity of this matter."

She stared at him. Her heart raced. Earlier, when she had roamed the woods, had she been past the barn? When he had come upon her, she hadn't been, but perhaps the woman in the woods had been, and she was what he wished to hide. "I must inquire as to the reason why?"

He took a deep breath. "I apologize, but I cannot offer an explanation." His eyes bore into her. "I realize this forces you to trust me implicitly and without question, are you able to do that?"

Her mind spun. "I—I—I'm unsure."

"I appreciate your honesty." He crossed his arms. "However, if I cannot trust you with this—"

She knew the meaning of his unspoken words—agree or leave.

But if she left, she'd forfeit her chance to help Elsie, and be near her brother.

"Do I have your assurance that there's nothing illegal or immoral occurring beyond that barn?"

A smile crept onto his face. "I most definitely can assure you of that. And if that is what has you concerned, you may take comfort in knowing that Pastor West is attuned to everything I do."

"That does offer some relief," she admitted.

"Good." His shoulders slackened. "I do believe this is best for all those involved." He gazed out into the distance, lost in his thoughts.

She eyed him with curiosity. She could live with this boundary rule, if—and only if—her brother resided within the limits.

"Where do you constrain your prisoners of war? Are they the reason we are not to venture past the barn?"

His head darted sideways. He scrutinized her. "They do reside in a log cabin on that section of my land. But please rest assured, you have nothing to fear from them."

She nodded. Did he include the woman in the woods as a prisoner of war? But if so, what had been her crime? Her stomach flipped. She abhorred the idea of confinement against her will. And yet, that would be the most civil treatment she could expect if he ever discovered her secret. She shuddered. Far worse consequences passed through her mind. For one, she could be hung. She rubbed her neck.

"You appear frightened. Please know you have nothing to fret about on their account." She drew her lips into

a tight smile and dipped her chin. He
didn't even possess an inkling of what
actually terrified her. "I keep my
prisoners of war either locked up or
under constant supervision, so once
more, please don't allow their
presence to distress you."

"I shall endeavor not to." She
looked at him evenly.

"Good. Because, as the nanny, you
shall encounter them."

She dipped her chin. "'Tis fine."
To all outward appearances she
remained resigned. However, inwardly,
she danced with delight. Visiting with
her brother would be better than fine,
'twas exactly what she had hoped for.

"Your words have now roused my
hope. Shall we celebrate your
acceptance of my terms of employment?"
He remained stoic until she nodded,
then a grin spread across his lips.
"We did sincerely pray you would
agree. Hence, we have a room lying in
wait of you. 'Tis located between
Elsie's bedroom and the one Halcyon,
our cook, shares with her husband,
Mickey. However, if Pastor West needs
you to remain with him—"

"I believe Pastor West can manage without me. He's seldom home. He devotes most of his time to visiting his parishioners. And I do believe I shall accomplish more here, helping Elsie."

He nodded. "When shall I tell Elsie to expect you?"

"To-morrow, after breakfast?"

"Perfect. Although knowing Elsie, she shall construe that as an eternity."

She laughed. "I do wish to discuss the matter with Pastor West and I shall need to gather my personal effects."

"Shall I come to collect you?"

"Nay, that shan't be necessary. And besides, you're notoriously busy."

He chuckled. "Then 'tis settled. Welcome, Penny." He held out his hand. She slid her fingers against his warm palm. But they didn't shake hands. Her eyes met his. She sucked in a breath. His grasp sent another shiver up her spine. This one however, was heartfelt, and pleasing.

But she ought not allow such feelings to linger. She snatched her hand away, and tucked a strand of hair behind her ear, as a pretext for her abrupt disengagement. Then she glanced down at an old tree stump to avoid his gaze. Only more trouble would ensue if she were to lose her heart to this man.

*   *   *

"I do thank you for bringing me, Pastor West." Penelope took the second valise he had wrenched from his wagon.

"My pleasure." He smiled down upon her. From behind him, the morning sun shot forth in every direction, as if he were in the center of a circle of divine light.

"But, although I shall miss your cheerful presence, I do agree, this is where you are needed most." She dipped her chin. "And I'm sorry I must leave posthaste. Please convey my apologies to Blair. There's a young couple I must meet with who are to wed this very Saturday." He stepped toward the front of his wagon. "Actually, it's Blair's cousin," he called over his shoulder.

"How lovely." She followed him. "But you need not apologize to me, and please do not look aggrieved. You have not forsaken me into the abyss. I shall be more than fine," she reassured him. "Once more, thank you for every kindness you've shown me." She patted his arm.

His gaze searched hers, as if he could see her innermost thoughts. She gulped, thankful he couldn't ascertain her secret.

"Do take care." He climbed up into his seat. "I shan't forgive myself if any harm befell you." He tipped his hat before he called to his horses and set off.

She raised her hand, but couldn't muster the strength to wave. Since the pastor knew not that P.J. was her brother, what *harm* did he suppose could befall her?

She watched the wagon struggle down the road. When 'twas out of sight, she let out a deep breath, then picked up her valises and lugged them toward Blair's house.

Did Pastor West possess knowledge of Blair's character that caused him

to be apprehensive? Her mind raced
back to her qualms about how hard
Blair had pushed her, and how he had
fought with that man on the sidewalk
the first day she had come to town.
Was he abusive? He was particularly
broad and muscular. And he was a
warden.

"You've arrived," Elsie shrieked,
after she had opened the front
entrance door.

Her thoughts scattered. "I have.
Good-day, Elsie." She entered and set
her valises down on the wood floor,
before she hugged Blair's niece with a
surge of tenderness. She had vowed to
fortify her heart against Blair, but
this little lass had already wormed
her way in, and she loved her all the
more for it.

"Uncle Blair directed me to show
you to your room first." Elsie pulled
away, and her demeanor turned into
someone ten years her elder.

"'Tis a fine suggestion." She
picked up her valises again and
trailed upstairs behind her hopping
and chattering charge. The joy Elsie
emitted was contagious, and soon her

trepidation dissipated. She smiled and listened to her with delight.

"This shall be your room." Elsie bounded in and jumped on the neatly arranged bed pushed into the corner. "Uncle Blair and I remembered how you fancied flowers. And even though I was terrified of another bee sting, I helped fill that entire vase." She beamed at the vanity table in front of the window where the flowers bloomed.

"Thank you." She lingered, to touch and smell every wildflower, hoping the lass wouldn't see a blush spread over her face. He had actually picked these for her? "They're beautiful," she choked.

"You are a princess," she laughed. "And yet you seem to be in a state of shock. I would think you'd be accustomed to such treatment."

She turned with her head shaking at Elsie. "Truly you do not believe I'm a princess, do you?"

"I most certainly do." She jumped from the bed. Her arms flailed dangerously close to the washbasin and pitcher that sat perched on the bedside table.

"Careful," her cautionary word came belatedly. Before she could stop Elsie, the lass' arm hit the pitcher.

"Oh, nay," Elsie cried, her words muffled in the crash. Terror struck her wee face as she stared at the shattered porcelain pieces. "Oh, nay," she repeated, as she swooped down to gather the remnants of the washbasin and pitcher.

"Elsie, stop." She ran to her. "You shall cut yourself." She grabbed hold of Elsie's frantic arms—too late. Her hands bled.

"I must clean away this mess." She shoved her tiny fingers back into the ragged pieces. "I must fix this."

"Nay, you must not." She pulled Elsie up onto her feet, then gripped hold of the squirming child and turned her away from the broken pieces.

Worse than a petrified horse, her eyes looked wild. "Elsie, calm yourself," she said, in a soothing, yet firm voice. "They were merely a washbasin and pitcher."

She shook her head, tears streamed down her cheeks. "I should have been more cautious. The fault is entirely mine. I'm sorry," she wailed.

"'Twas an accident. Please, calm yourself." She held her shaking body tighter, unable to comprehend why she trembled in terror. "I shall set this to rights," she assured her. "But first we need to tend to your cuts." She examined the crimson covered hands. "Pray tell, why would you touch the shards?"

Her eyes widened. Her lips quivered. Whatever thoughts frightened her she wouldn't share. Penelope's ire rose. Who had instilled such fear into this child?

*　　*　　*

Penelope's heart charged fiercer than a herd of bison. "Blair, I must speak with you." She stormed into the corridor as soon as she heard him enter the house.

He stood with his back to her as he hung his hat, unaware of the steam that had erupted from her. "I apologize for missing my midday meal, but the amount of work to be done this day grew in enormity as the day progressed." He casually hit some dirt off his trousers. "I am however early for supper, that ought to count for something." His lips were curled as he turned, but his smile vanished the moment he saw her seething with anger. "Is something amiss?" Concern creased his brow.

"Aye." She folded her arms. "There most certainly is. May I speak with you privately?" She leaned her weight from one leg to the other, impatiently awaiting his answer.

"Certainly," his voice cracked. "In my study?" She gave him a curt nod, then marched into the aforesaid room. "Please, sit." He motioned to the golden eagle colored sofa near his desk.

But she could not sit. She could scarcely contain her anger. She paced, as he closed the door. "Blair, I must speak with you regarding Elsie."

"Has she been into mischief?" He sauntered to his desk, his tone entirely too flippant.

Her fists tightened and her irritation bubbled to the surface. *"Has she been into mischief*? Do you believe the child to be a miscreant who continuously misbehaves?"

He stood before his desk chair. "Nay." He eyed her. "But you appear furious, and since you were her companion this entire day, I cannot think of another reason for your irritation."

"Indeed?" She charged his desk. "And are you in constant agitation regarding her behavior?"

"Nay." His eyes narrowed. However, she wasn't about to be deterred.

"Honestly?"

"Aye." He mimicked her with crossed arms. "Pray tell, what does this pertain to?"

Her eyes drilled into his. "Earlier, Elsie broke the pitcher and washbasin in my room." She paused to assess his anger. However, his composure didn't alter. He didn't even flinch, let alone clench his jaw, and not one bead of sweat appeared on his forehead. "Perhaps you failed to hear me?"

"Sorry." He leaned on his desk. "Was anyone hurt?"

"Aye." Her hands hit her hips. "Elsie cut her hands as she tried to clean her mess."

"Is she in terrible pain?" His eyebrows slammed together.

"I bandaged her, and I do believe she shall heal soon enough—"

"Good." He straightened to his full height, and rolled his head from side to side to remove the stiffness from his neck. "I'm sorry she gave you such a fright."

"Pardon me?" She grimaced. "'Twas not I who was frightened, 'twas her."

He looked at her quizzically. "I would expect as much since she cut herself."

"That is not what frightened her," her harsh tone hitched his eyebrow up. "That little lass shook with a fear for her life because she had broken something."

"Ah," he breathed out his remark with several nods as he settled into his chair. "And you assumed I might be the cause of such dreadful fear?"

Aye. She stared at him, but didn't utter that word aloud, because as she regarded his troubled expression, she realized he had remained calm this whole time, and the first thoughts of doubt appeared in her mind. Had she misinterpreted the entire situation?

"I suppose 'tis high time I disclosed her past." He rubbed the back of his neck. She sat on the edge of the sofa that faced him. "Her father was a violent man."

Her heart constricted. That poor tiny creature.

"Elsie has never been keen to discuss him, and I shan't force her. I simply reckon she'll talk when she's ready."

She nodded. "'Tis such a relief to know she's not in fear of you. I apologize for my interrogation, Blair, but the anguish in her eyes was—"

"Too much to contend with?"

She dipped her chin.

"I fully understand. However, you need not apologize. I'm rather pleased, and impressed, you confronted me. This provides me further assurance you care more for her well-being than your own. And I thank you for that, as I too abhor the thought of her tormented. But her father's gone now, and I pray she shall heal in due time."

"Aye." Her body tensed as her mind reeled. "But even though she may heal, she may never forget."

His gaze fixed on her. "Do you speak from experience?"

"Unfortunately, I do." She rubbed her hands together. "My years at that orphan asylum were grim." She fought to hold her memories at bay, but she couldn't refuse how his inquisitive eyes beseeched her. "I lived in permanent terror of receiving reprimands for wrongdoings, perceived or otherwise." She looked into the empty hearth. "Even the tiniest, most obscure infraction, such as an untied shoelace, resulted in a whipping."

She gazed back at him. A rush of admiration inundated her. He had saved Elsie from a similar fate. However, she reminded herself, he was her brother's warden. He might be her brother's tormentor. She couldn't fall in love with him.

"I shan't detain you any longer." She stood abruptly. His head snapped up. His fingers flew to rub a new kink at the back of his neck. "But I must entreat you with one additional request." She stepped toward his desk. "May I have use of a wagon to-morrow to travel into town to purchase another pitcher and washbasin?"

"You mustn't drain your finances to replace my possessions." He came around the desk. "However, if you wish to choose the articles that suit you, I'd welcome your company."

His nearness disconcerted her better sense—but only for a moment. She stepped back. "I'm certain you are fully capable of handling such matters without my assistance."

"True, but I certainly shall benefit from a woman's opinion—*your* opinion."

Her mouth gaped. Then somehow, a murmur came forth, "'Twould be my honor."

"Nay, 'twould be entirely mine."
His eyes held hers. She studied them,
especially how the light played with
the brown flecks, softening them so
they appeared copper.

Stop, she commanded herself. She
shouldn't be cognizant of such things.
She averted her gaze. However, their
connection didn't break. He still
regarded her intently. "Would you care
to visit with Elsie before supper?"
She spun toward the door.

"Aye," he replied after a
moment's pause, then strode to open
the door for her.

"She's in the drawing room
playing with her dolls." She walked
ahead, his footfalls just behind hers.
The knowledge of his eyes fixed on her
person nearly caused her knees to
buckle. But she shan't trip, she
scolded herself, as she rushed into
the drawing room. "Elsie, your uncle
wishes to visit with you," she
announced, then stood to the side
allowing him to pass.

"Magnificent," she beamed and ran
to him.

"I shall leave you alone." She retreated into the doorway. His nearness had blurred her senses. She desperately needed to garner some distance.

"You need not leave," he offered, his words a hoarse whisper since he stood exceedingly close.

His proposal touched her. But she shook her head. "Thank you, but if 'tis all the same to you, I shall see you at supper." When he didn't protest, she bowed from the room. Once out of sight, she held her chest, as if that action would prevent her heart from attaching itself to him. She trudged outside and took a deep breath. She desperately needed to right her senses.

When she opened her eyes she saw Halcyon had exited the kitchen. The cook awkwardly tried to balance three plates of food. She rushed to her aid and reached for a tottering plate. "Please, allow me."

"Thank ye, but I can manage." The older woman twisted to avoid her hand. The plate tipped, then fell from her grasp.

"I insist." She grabbed the plate mid-air.

"Thank ye," the cook grumbled. "Normally, I deliver these in two outings, but with those dark clouds rolling in I fear being caught in a storm."

"I hadn't noticed." She looked to see that indeed the inclement weather was steadily approaching. "We'd best hurry."

"Aye." Halcyon walked on. "Wait." She stopped. "I distinctly remember Blair issued an order that ye weren't supposed to travel past the barn."

"Correct." Her eyes wandered to the barn. "Are you to journey thus far?" Reluctantly, the cook nodded. "And are you acquainted with the details as to why I'm not allowed past the barn?"

She laughed. "If I did, I wouldn't tell ye."

Interesting. Halcyon, along with Pastor West, and most likely, Halcyon's husband, Mickey, knew what Blair kept past the barn. Why were her and Elsie not permitted to know?

"I understand." Her heart skipped with an urge to run past the barn and discover the secret. "Then I shall only carry these as far as the barn."

"Thank ye." Halcyon moved forward once more.

"To whom are you bringing these plates?" she asked, as she kept pace with the nearly running cook.

"Never, ye, mind," Halcyon snorted with a stern look. "Ye would do well to remember yer place."

She nodded.

"Pardon me." Halcyon stopped after a stretch of considerable silence. "'Tis not my intention to be unpleasant, but I have my orders. And trust me, ye don't wish to know. I wish I wasn't privy."

Penelope studied her. She appeared sincere. "I believe you."

"Good." Halcyon smiled. "We best continue," her words were illuminated with a flash of lightning and Penelope hurried alongside her.

"The wind is certainly gaining force." Halcyon shook her head to relieve herself of the annoying strands of hair that whipped her face.

"Aye." She dipped her head to push against the wind's strength.

"I do believe we've lost the fight against time," Halcyon called over the whistling wind. Penelope glanced up at the gloomy, dark sky. "Blair ought to understand why I sent ye to bring those suppers to the prisoners of war. But then ye must return straight back to the house, ye hear?"

Her head shot to Halcyon. All thoughts of Halcyon's destination vanished. Finally, a chance to see her brother.

"**I** promise I shall return to the house," Penelope steadied her voice, even though her insides threatened to jump out of her body. *Thank You, God, for providing me with the chance to see my brother.*

A crack of thunder jolted her. "Their cabin is just over yonder." Halcyon pointed, after she handed her a second plate. "Now, make haste. I don't wish fer either of us to be struck by lightning." She bustled into the forest. Penelope tried to look past her, but couldn't see a thing besides the trees. Was she disappearing to that woman in the woods?

Another thunderclap shook her. She spun on her heel and hurried toward her brother's cabin. "Supper," she shouted when she neared the locked door. She rested one of the plates on a ledge.

"Halcyon? Are you ill?" A man's voice erupted from within.

"Nay, Clyde. Halcyon is elsewhere." She prayed her brother wouldn't succumb to shock at the sound of her voice. He couldn't reveal her identity.

"Then who is speaking?" the man demanded. "And how, pray tell, do you know my name?"

She sucked in a breath thinking how to respond. She couldn't simply admit that sheer deduction equated to his voice not belonging to her brother. "We met at church. You wished for me to take a turn with you."

"Am I to believe that such a fashionable, pretty lady now delivers my supper?" his voice softened. "How, or better yet, why?"

"This inclement weather. I'm merely helping Halcyon. I'm the new nanny."

"And your name is—" he elongated the last word with husky flirtation.

"Penelope Sherwood," she answered, then waited with abated breath for her brother's reaction.

"Penelope?" P.J. spit. A clamor ensued. He must have sprung to his feet.

"Calm yourself, man," Clyde shouted. "That chair nearly hit me."

"Sorry." Her brother approached the door.

Clyde grunted at him. "Your face is as white as snow. Are you acquainted with my church beauty?"

He didn't answer. She held her breath. Her brother wasn't one to lie. "Hey, men," she summoned their attention. "Am I supposed to slide these plates through this thin opening?"

"Aye," they answered in unison.

"Here's the first one then." She pushed the plate through. One of them took it.

"A feast, as usual," Clyde rasped. "Please give our compliments to Halcyon."

"I shall." She slid the second plate through. "There's to be a storm soon, are you both fine?" Surely her brother would understand her true meaning and elaborate.

"Fine, is not the term I would use," Clyde retorted. Her heart sank at the thought of P.J. having suffered. "Being locked in a one room log cabin is not what I would deem *fine*. I have only two sets of clothes, my British uniform for visiting town, and these horrid rags for working on the farm—"

"Never mind Clyde, Penny—elope," her brother stumbled over her name.

"We're fine. Our lodging and effects are comfortable enough."

"Comfortable?" Clyde bellowed. "My mansion in Upper Canada is *comfortable*." She heard a clang and assumed Clyde had thrown his supper plate on a table before he strutted back to the door. "Perhaps after this war ends you shall do me the honor of visiting me there, Penelope?"

"Clyde," P.J. growled.

"Don't chide me," the man sneered, then lowered his voice. "Perhaps you haven't had the pleasure of regarding just how beautiful this woman is."

"Penny." Her name came from behind. "Pray tell, why are ye still here?" Halcyon ran toward her. "Ye should have been at the house by now. Make haste. The rain shall not wait fer ye."

"Of course." She held in a sigh, not wishing to move. Let the rain soak her through, she'd gladly risk lightning for more time with her brother.

"Good night, men," Halcyon called out. "We're in fer a storm so brace

yerselves. I shall return with yer
morning meal."

"Good night," the men answered,
as Halcyon grabbed her hand and
dragged her running home for shelter.

"I see them," Elsie screeched
from her perch by the window.

Blair opened the curtain wider to
peer out even farther. "Finally,
they've come," he mumbled. He'd been
doing his best to present a nonchalant
exterior for his niece's sake. Since
her parents' accident her likelihood
of reacting hysterically to situations
such as these was far from uncommon.
But he couldn't temper the beating of
his own heart, he'd prayed for Penny's
safe return just as much as his niece.
"There now, Elsie, is it not always
wise to entrust your worries to God?"

"Aye," she conceded.

He put his arm around her. "Penny
is well. She merely accompanied
Halcyon. And they shall both be safe
indoors before the rain begins."

She nodded. "They certainly do
run fast."

"Indeed, they do." His gaze remained fixed on Penny. She held her skirts up just high enough for her dainty shoes to quickly traverse the land. The strong wind whipped her blonde hair about, and blew her dress into her. She stole his breath.

"Uncle Blair," Elsie bawled. His every muscle tightened as Penny's foot dipped into a ditch and she tumbled to the ground. "Is she hurt?"

"Wait here." He darted from the room.

The wind slapped him as he ran to where Halcyon helped Penny stand. She winced in pain when she attempted to put weight on her left foot.

"Are ye able to walk?" Halcyon asked. Penny leaned on her and nodded, but winced when she placed her foot down.

He grabbed hold of her from the other side. She gasped. Whether due to his touch, or more pain, lay uncertain. Although, he couldn't permit himself to dwell upon it. Large raindrops thumped down. "We must move indoors. May I carry you?"

"I can walk—oh," she cried.

"Allow him to carry ye lass before we're all killed," Halcyon shouted.

"Fine," Penny consented.

He picked her up and ran into the house as the storm unleashed its fury.

"You're soaked through," Elsie frowned, as he carried her into the corridor. He didn't wish such wetness for her health, but her newfound state gave him the opportunity to see her in a new light. And she was beautiful, glistening with raindrops.

Halcyon shook her clothes. "Aye, Elsie. We most certainly are sodden."

"Penny, are you terribly hurt?" Elsie struggled to move closer to them, but Halcyon unknowingly bared her progress. "We witnessed your fall." She leaned sideways to peer around the cook. "Uncle Blair, please set Penny down here." She patted the settee in the corridor nearest her.

"Of course." He understood the lass' need to be near her and couldn't begrudge her, even though he knew he'd feel a dreadful sense of loss the moment his contact with Penny ceased. And sure enough, as soon as he placed her down, a coolness expanded over his chest where her warm body had been pressed, and that loss quickly spread over the rest of him.

"Perhaps I may have sprained my ankle a wee bit, but I assure you there's nothing whatsoever to fret about. A good night's rest shall see it right." She ran her hand over Elsie's hair.

"If ye'll excuse me, I best change, then get supper on the table." Halcyon smacked her clothes as she sauntered toward the kitchen.

"Do you wish to retire to your room?" he asked Penny. He would not be bothered in the least to have her in his arms once more if she needed to be carried up the stairs.

"Nay, I believe this July heat shall see me dry soon enough. But I do wish to thank you for carrying me indoors. If you hadn't, my limp would have either overwhelmed Halcyon or left us stranded. And I thank you for saving me from the guilt of that. She's terrified of being struck by lightning."

He dipped his chin. He wasn't
certain if he'd seen a flash of
lightning or if he'd merely seen a
glow when her eyes had met his.
Nevertheless, a bolt of electricity
had shot through him.

"Uncle Blair, you're the
princess' knight in shining armor."
She gazed up at him with enchantment,
then turned to Penny. "Is he not a
most dashing knight?"

Penny's rosy lips curled slowly
then spread into a full grin. "Aye, he
is. You're one lucky lass to have him
as your uncle."

His chest swelled with her words.
If only she would consider herself
lucky to be his one day.

*   *   *

Penelope grimaced at her
reflection in the looking glass. She
ought not be this concerned with her
appearance. They were merely visiting
town to shop. Blair was not a
gentleman caller. This was not an
afternoon stroll. *He's an American.*

Your brother's warden, she scolded herself.

However, that didn't cease the flutter in her stomach when his knuckles rapped on her bedroom door. "Are you prepared to leave?"

"Aye." She bounded from her chair and opened the door.

"Elsie's downstairs helping Halcyon." He hitched his thumb toward the stairs. "I just left them."

She smiled and twiddled her closed parasol. "I hope you don't mind, but Elsie wished to remain here and help Halcyon bake pies."

"She is determined to someday learn how to make her favourite dessert all by herself." He chuckled, then stepped back to allow her to join him in the corridor. "Before we go—" he hesitated at the top of the stairs "—I need to make an amendment to our plans. I do hope you shan't be vexed by my insistence?"

She stared at him. Did he wish this excursion to be more than a mere shopping excursion, as well? "Pray tell?" her voice squeaked, despite her best effort to exude calmness.

"I must bring along one of my prisoners to help me load the wagon with supplies."

"Oh." She nodded. "Of course." She squeezed her parasol tighter. "'Tis perfectly reasonable."

"You're not upset?" He eyed her. "Because you appear a wee bit uneasy."

"Nay, nay. I'm not bothered in the least." She smiled up at him. What had she foolishly hoped? *Silly creature!*

"Are you certain? Because I shan't wish you to be uncomfortable."

"I shan't be," she reassured him. "I am British, after all." And in fact, if the prisoner was her brother, she'd be elated.

"Good, because I've always argued that as long as my prisoners remain respectful, aren't violent, and follow my rules, they ought to be able to associate with those in the community."

"Is that why you take them along with you to church?"

He nodded. "That, and 'tis in the parole agreement they signed." His grin widened.

She squinted. This was her chance to probe. To ask the myriad of questions that until now she hadn't been able to broach. "But they're your enemies, shouldn't you wish to have them remain locked up, or punished, or put to death?"

He shook his head. "'Twasn't too long ago that the United States was British. And although this is our second war with Britain, many of those who live in Upper Canada were Loyalists who emigrated there after the War of Independence. They're some of our relatives and friends, people we shan't wish to hurt." He leaned against the stair rail. "Unfortunately, however, not everyone stands in agreement with me."

"Nay?" she asked, knowing full well the hate that dwelled in some people's hearts.

He laughed. "I shall spare you the vulgarities that I must listen to."

"Thank you." She grinned. "That is most kind of you."

He immediately understood her overstated gratitude and dipped his head with exaggeration, then motioned for them to descend the stairs. "As you know, there aren't enough prisons in the whole of the United States to hold all these prisoners of war, hence the duty of guarding them falls on people such as myself, and 'tis my opinion that if we treat our prisoners well, we should be able to expect the same for those Americans captured by the British." He shot a glance over his shoulder. His eyes radiated sincerity. "And whilst I have loved ones fighting in this war, I do what I can, in hope that kindness shall be extended to them if need be."

She nodded, profusely agreeing with his reasoning. Her shoulders lightened. P.J. had said he was *comfortable* here. *God, I shan't be able to control how loudly I sing Your praises if Blair's words mean that he has been treating P.J. well.*

"Nevertheless, even though I aim to be fair, human nature is what it is, and I must remember that these men are my prisoners. I do need to treat them accordingly."

The heaviness sank back onto her shoulders. "Do you beat them?" She stopped on the bottom step. He turned and look at her. She had to know what P.J.'s fate had been.

"I haven't found the need to and hope I never shall." He crossed his arms. "But you've met Clyde. He is certainly a good deal to contend with." She nodded, unable to fully breathe whilst she fretted about her brother. "I must remain on guard at all times with him, because I'm uncertain what he's capable of, and because of that, I must treat my other prisoner, Paul, with more severity than I believe he deserves."

She swallowed hard. "Do you fear for your life?" Her eyes fell on the pistol he always strapped to his side.

"Every single minute. I cannot allow anyone to take me from Elsie. She cannot be left to fend for herself."

Unlike how her parents had abandoned them as children. Her heart gladdened for Elsie, and she stepped down the remaining stair. "I'm sorry." She touched his forearm. She understood the responsibility and stress he constantly dealt with.

He looked down upon her hand, then back into her eyes. A grin spread across his face. "Please, don't fret. I'm capable in my capacity as a warden. And Clyde shan't be accompanying us. Paul agreed, and he's never given me cause for concern. Not that I would ever let anything happen to you."

She dipped her chin. Words failed her after his protective assertion. If only she could tell him he was correct. He had absolutely nothing to fear from her brother, because P.J. was a true gentleman.

"Shall we?"

"We shall." She walked out of the house ahead of him, as he held the door open.

With an enormous grin and a wink to her brother, who thankfully remained picturesque, she stopped before the wagon, knowing full well that Blair hadn't seen the enthusiasm she had just gushed at her brother.

However, she knew she would need to strive hard not to allow her familiarity and love for her brother to venture forth. If P.J. was supposed to be a stranger, she must behave as such. She must make certain Blair never suspected a thing.

To begin, she would need to remember to call her brother, Paul, not P.J. Because only the two of them knew they were related. They didn't even share the same surname. She had taken her adopted parents' name and P.J. had kept their surname from the orphan asylum. The people of Upper Canada didn't even know P.J.'s surname, because their adopted parents had always referred to him as a Sherwood. And thankfully, every time the pastor or his daughter had come to Newark, they'd never once met P.J. or saw a likeness of him hanging on the wall.

"Hello." She turned away from her brother, who sat in the back.

"Hello," he responded, and looked away from her, as well, whilst Blair helped her into her seat.

"Thank you," she courteously jested. He smiled, then released her hand, before he loped around the front of the horses and climbed aboard.

"I welcome the opportunity to sit and view the countryside," P.J. remarked as the horses trotted their familiar route. "The view is much better whilst resting than working."

Blair laughed. "I agree." He glanced at the vastness that surrounded them.

"Do you work alongside one another?" she asked. Out of the corner of her eye she glanced at Blair.

"Aye." His concentration didn't leave the road.

"Oh," surprise rushed from her.

"Aye, not many wardens do as much," her brother added.

"Nay, I suppose not." Her gaze remained fixed on Blair.

"I know if Clyde were the warden and Blair the prisoner, Clyde would gladly order Blair about whilst he sat in the shade sipping a beverage," her brother smirked and Blair nodded in amused agreement.

"Are there many prisoners of war in the area?" she asked, hoping to keep this topic of conversation open to discern all she could about her brother's well-being.

"Not in our town," Blair answered. "Most British officers are sent farther south, away from the border, and those of lower rank, are kept mainly in barracks, under conditions you would deem deplorable."

"Oh." She fidgeted in her seat. "Then do you consider yourself fortunate to have been sent here, Paul?" She straightened her skirt.

"Aye." He coughed, and she knew he thought she sounded overly concerned. She must reign in her emotions. "I believe God not only blessed me by keeping me alive during this war, but He sent me to the one man I believe may be the fairest of wardens."

Her heart leapt with joy. She peered over her right shoulder at a passing pond to hide her face from Blair. Her brother had clearly known what she had meant to ask, and she thanked God he had told her precisely what she had wished to hear.

"Thank you, Paul." Blair glanced at him. "But unfortunately, I'm not worthy of the title."

Her head jerked toward Blair. "Why ever not?"

His eyes met hers. His smile faded as he spoke, "I fear I've neglected to aid Paul in sending letters home in a more timely manner. He's only sent one letter home thus far."

"I'm certain most wardens never even permit their prisoners that consideration," her brother interposed, and she was glad P.J. had succeeded in pulling Blair's attention from her zealous outburst.

"Perhaps not, but I do wish to rectify my oversight," he responded.

"How kind of you," her voice purred demurely.

He shrugged and dismissed her admiration. "I ought to have offered some time ago. But, perhaps now that I've employed a nanny to lessen my burdens, life shall improve for all involved." He flashed her a smile. "I'd be happy to send a letter to your family, as well."

"That's not necessary," her words raced forth. She couldn't allow him to discover that her address matched P.J.'s. "But I thank you," she slowed her words and studied the creases around his genuinely concerned eyes.

"We have become exceedingly good at thanking one another, have we not?" He winked, which sent a shiver up her spine.

She laughed, "We have definitely improved immensely."

"I had a sister who was never partial to saying *thank you*," P.J. joked. "Although, I shouldn't say *had*, she is still very much alive."

"Let me assure you, Paul, if Penny and I can learn to say thank you more often, then your sister can be taught, as well." She smiled at Blair before her gaze dropped to her lap. Her gut wrenched at having such a conversation racked with double meanings. *God, help me. I hate living under this guise.*

"Aye," P.J. spoke with a smile. "My sister truly is the sweetest. I thank God He chose her to be my little sister."

"You must miss her," Blair lost the playfulness in his tone. "I confess to missing mine."

"I'm sorry," P.J. responded. "I would be devastated if I ever lost my sister. I do pray she's never in the path of misfortune. I couldn't bear to see her hurt. Hopefully when I write, she shall alleviate my worry by telling me she's where she ought to be, safe at home during this war."

Her stomach sank. She didn't wish to cause him any agony.

"Penny is away from her home in Newark, and she's out of harm's way." Blair's attempt to soothe P.J.'s turmoil touched her heart. "You must trust that wherever your sister is, she's safe, as well."

"I do hope you're correct." P.J. eyed her. "I must trust she has enough sense to keep herself safe."

"I'm sure she does," Blair continued. Her shoulders sank. "And we shall send your letter posthaste so you may lay your fears to rest."

"Thank you." P.J. sat back.

She silently watched the town approach. Her mind raced. She thanked

God her brother hadn't been tortured. However, now she must break his heart and tell him about their pa's death. Then she'd be without a reason to stay—except for Elsie. She looked at the handsome man beside her—and Blair. She sighed.

"Thank you," Penelope exaggerated the words that had become such an intimate joke between her and Blair. His eyes danced with mirth as he held the door to the general store door open. His considerate ways were entirely too easy to become accustomed to. She clearly needed to distance herself.

"Good day," she returned the proprietor's salutation, then left Blair to inquire into his purchases, as she sauntered to the far end of the store to examine some linens.

She prayed she would get a chance to speak with her brother privately, but he stood beside Blair. Soon he offered to carry Blair's purchases to the wagon. Her hopes were dashed. She would just need to find another occasion—or perhaps she could excuse herself and meet with him alone by the wagon. She smiled at her new plan, turned abruptly, then walked directly toward Blair.

The sun shone through the large front window and revealed lighter strands in his brown hair. He stood leaning over the counter, deep in a pleasant conversation with the proprietor. Nevertheless, as she approached, he straightened. She swallowed, noticing again how much muscle he had under his command. "Did you take a fancy to anything in particular?"

Aye, *you.* She smiled. *And if I'm not more careful my fancy for you shall overwhelm me.* She bit her tongue. 'Twould never do to harbor such a fondness for him.

"You retain exceptionally fine wares," she turned her smile upon the proprietor.

"Thank you," he replied, then faced Blair once more. "Allow me to determine whether I have any in stock."

He dipped his chin. "Much obliged." The man left as Blair turned and leaned against the counter. "Is that washbasin to your liking?" He pointed.

She followed his gaze. "'Tis lovely. And proves my help wasn't needed." With a smile, she looked up into his deep brown eyes. She knew full well she ought not to have. She clasped her hands together and turned her attention out the front window to watch P.J.

As soon as the proprietor returned, she'd politely excuse herself and join her brother. "Oh, nay," she shouted, and instinctively grabbed Blair's forearm. "Are you acquainted with those men?" Fear choked her. She gasped. "What are they playing at?" She stepped forward. She wouldn't watch in frozen terror. However, before she moved another step, Blair had already bounded out and P.J. fell to the ground.

od, help them. Penelope bolted from the general store. P.J. fought with one man, after Blair pulled the second assailant off him.

"Filthy British officer." The man sank his fist into her brother's face.

"Leave him alone," Blair shouted, then defended himself from a blow to the stomach. "He's my prisoner of war, you're unauthorized."

"He's an enemy. He deserves to die." The man's rage boiled over. He and Blair traded blows.

"Nay, he doesn't. We're all God's children, you're not entitled to make such a decision." Blair kept his eyes locked on the man as fists pounded flesh and blood spilled forth.

She charged to Blair's side, intent to end this fight. "Penny, leave here at once," he shouted. The moment he turned to shield her, a fist knocked painfully into his jaw.

Her heart skipped with guilt. She never meant to cause him harm. This must end. Now. She reached forward and grabbed the cold metal object he had attached to his waist, before Blair thrust himself against the man once more. Swiftly, she raised her hands above her head and fired the pistol.

Her hands shook from the power she'd unleashed, and when she brought her arms down, the men had backed away.

"We don't want trouble," one of them said, his palms in the air. His appearance struck a chord of familiarity. Was he the man Blair had fought after they'd first met?

"You *don't want trouble*?" She rushed forward a few steps. "That isn't the impression I received."

"Penny, my pistol." Fear lined Blair's face as he held out his hand. Did he actually think she would shoot these men? A smile licked her lips. She turned back to the two assailants and waved the pistol at them.

"Not until we settle this matter once and for all." She glared at the two men. "I understand we're at war, but as Blair articulated, we are all children of God, understand?" The men nodded. "Then you shall allow Blair to handle his prisoners of war the way he deems fit, without your interference?"

"Aye," they answered in unison. She prayed they'd spoken the truth. "Make yourselves scarce then." She waved them away with the pistol. They didn't hesitate.

"May I please have my pistol back now?" Blair steamed hotter than the metal in her hand.

"Certainly." She gladly handed the weapon to him. She may know how to use a pistol, but that didn't mean she enjoyed it.

"Pray tell, why did you behave in such a manner? You could have killed someone," he fumed.

"The only creature I could have killed was a bird flying by at an inopportune time." She grimaced. "Now, I think 'tis only fair that you say *thank you*. I did just rid us of them, permanently, I hope."

She stood firmly in front of him. His lips twitched upward. "You certainly don't fail to amaze me, Miss Sherwood." He shook his head with a laugh. "The more I believe I have deciphered your person, the more you combat my misconceptions."

"Good." She grinned. "But enough about that. Are either of you seriously hurt?"

She scrutinized his face, and body. And although she attempted to perform her examination with a medical eye, she was not a doctor, and had to avert her gaze. He was truly a man to behold. She swallowed, her throat drier than dust.

"I'm fine," his husky voice hauled her out of her thoughts and brought her eyes back up to his. He'd withstood the physical assault with only minor cuts and scrapes that may bruise, but those somehow enhanced his handsome, brawn features.

"Good." She turned away from him. "Paul?" Her brother's nose dripped with blood. Her chest constricted. "P—Paul," she corrected herself as she raced to him. "You're hurt."

"Nay, nay, I'm fine." He stared at her. Immediately she understood her mistake. She had behaved in an overly concerned manner. "'Tis only my nose that bleeds."

"Here. Take my handkerchief," she forced the words out, then stood back. She hugged herself to keep her limbs from throwing themselves around him.

"Whilst you were outnumbered, they certainly issued you a severe beating." Blair came to assess her brother. "You ought to sit." To her relief, he put his arm around him and helped him into the wagon. "I apologize, Paul. That's not my first troublesome encounter with one of those men, but I shall speak with the sheriff, because I do wish this to be the last." P.J. dipped his chin, then sat in such a manner that instinctively showed her he was experiencing immense pain. "And I shall order you and Clyde another set of clothes, much finer than those you work in on the farm, so you may don something other than your British uniforms when you travel into town."

"Thank you." Her brother attempted a smile.

Blair dipped his chin. "I'm sorry, I ought to have foreseen this. I shall order them posthaste. Hopefully, they shall be completed in a fortnight."

"Much appreciated." P.J. examined his sores, as Blair turned to her and held out his hand to help her into her seat. "Please, excuse me, I shall only be a moment more in the store, then we shall return home."

She nodded. But when her skin touched his, she gripped his fingers tight and turned her chin up to look directly into his eyes. "Thank you for helping my br—" his eyebrows pulled together. She bit her lower lip. She'd nearly revealed her secret, yet again. *Utter foolishness!* "—brethren. Him being a fellow *British* citizen and all." She continued to spew words to disguise her fluster, "I too believe we are all children of God."

He dipped his chin. "I live by that thought and treat people as such."

"A most excellent way to live." She delighted in the darker brown specks of his eyes, and saw within them the gentleness and caring he possessed.

He was not obliged to aid her brother, especially since doing so placed him in harm's way, and yet, he had. He'd stated his belief in fairness, and treating people with kindness, and thus far, she'd witnessed nothing besides his complete exemplification of those principles.

And she couldn't be more grateful. If he hadn't helped her brother—she didn't wish to even imagine the calamity that may have befallen P.J. "Even though I'm certain your assistance to Paul was not performed for glory, I do wish you to know you're a hero in my eyes."

"Thank you. But if you allot me such a title, you must accept the title of heroine." He squeezed her hand back and helped her up into the wagon. "I shall only be but a moment."

She shook his words away. He had merely reflected her compliment back. Nothing more. "Do you fare any better?" she asked P.J, devoid of the overly protective concern that would have flowed more naturally.

"I'm fine."

They sat in silence and watched Blair until he entered the general store. "Please reassure me you're not dreadfully hurt?" She forced herself not to turn in her seat.

"As I said before, I'm fine. You mustn't concern yourself with me or you risk revealing our relationship. And I certainly do not wish to know

what shall happen to us then? I've
heard of, and unfortunately seen,
prisoners escape, only to be
recaptured and then beaten, thrown
into dungeons, deprived of food and
water, or threatened with death." She
shivered. "We could both be sentenced
to hang if anyone thought you were
here to help me escape." The terror in
his voice knotted her stomach.

"Penny, you must understand that
in war too many senseless acts happen,
and since I intend to make it out of
this war alive, along with you, you
must promise me you shall never allow
Blair, or anyone else, to discern our
connection."

"I shan't. I promise."

"Good, because I fear the
consequences. And besides, unless it
has slipped your notice, Blair is a
good man, and I thank, God, He sent me
here. I shan't wish to alter my
circumstances."

Aye, she had begun to realize
exactly how tremendous a man Blair
McAllister was, and thus, how
fortunate her brother was. "I do
indeed attempt with the utmost caution

not to fret openly where you are
concerned, but 'tis alarmingly
difficult. Although, I shall bolster
my efforts. But please, whence we
arrive home, do allow Halcyon to tend
to you. Your appearance is reminiscent
of a carcass that's been pecked over
by a flock of ravenous birds."

"Thanks," he jeered.

"Sorry." She shrugged with a
smile. "You may claim to be well, but
I know you're simply trying to say
what shan't distress me. You've always
been protective of me."

"Me? Protective of you?" He
laughed without moving his lips to
avoid annoying his injuries. "Are you
not the one who risked entering enemy
territory to find me?"

"Fair enough." She wiped a tear
from the corner of her eye. "But as
infants, we were abandoned with only
each other to rely on, and without
you, I shan't have survived." She
shuddered. "That orphan asylum—"

"I know," his soothing voice
hugged her. She glanced back at
him—at the scar that lay forevermore
etched across his right cheek when he

took the blame, and punishment, for something she'd been wrongfully accused of. "I shan't have survived without you, either. You were the sole reason I never succumbed way to despair."

"Likewise." She squeezed her hands in her lap. "And now we're united in this, and we shall both leave here alive, as well."

"But we ought not to be united in this, Penny. Your life ought to never have been in peril."

"I understand the dangers, but I had to come."

"Why?"

She took a deep breath. "Pa requested this of me."

"Incomprehensible! Pray tell, why?"

She took another deep breath. "If only another opportunity to speak alone could be assured, because I certainly do not wish to tell you in this manner."

"You must speak now. This may be our only occasion," her brother urged. "Please, make haste, Blair may return at any moment."

She bit her lip, squeezed her eyes shut and tried to summon the courage. "Please brace yourself, this pertains to pa."

"Proceed, please," he said, but his voice rattled.

"Pa died."

"Nay." He shook his head.

"I'm sorry." Her eyes misted. Her pain deepened from not being able to embrace her brother. "In May, Pa fell ill, and perhaps due to his age or other circumstances, by the end of the month, he didn't recover."

"How's mama?"

"You may imagine the depth of her grief. However, she has now stabilized and is coping as well as one can under such circumstances. My friend, Jamilyn, the pastor's daughter, dwells at our house for companionship whilst I'm here."

"Good, I'm glad to hear of it. I wouldn't wish mama to be alone. But we must cease our discussion," he hissed. "Blair may be upon us at any moment."

"Aye." She straightened the front of her bib-closing empire waist gown. She ought to appear as if she hadn't spoken with him—but, "I must disclose what Pa adamantly declared on his death bed. He wished to apologize to you."

"Apologize to me? Whatever for?"

"For his insistence on purchasing your post as an officer. He never dreamt a war would ensue. He simply wished for you to own the status rank that such a post provided. I dare say, guilt gnawed at him."

"Indeed, I wish it never had. I'm truly thankful for every attention he and mama paid us. And now—" he paused "—I shan't ever tell him so."

"Don't lament," she soothed him. "I spoke for you. I knew your heart, and conveyed as much. However, he still insisted I come. He wished me to ensure you fared well. I assured him I would, and I do believe 'tis the reason he died in peace."

"Then, I'm most glad for your presence."

"If not for pa, I should still have come," she smirked. "I do love you."

"I know," he tittered. "I love you, as well. And I ought to have expected as much after I sent that letter home."

"You know me well." She smiled to herself. "There is nothing I would not do for you."

"Truly?" Her brother leaned forward.

"Of course."

"Good. Then as your brother, I insist you go home."

"Home?" A dull ache in her head announced itself. "But I've scarcely just arrived. Surely you cannot expect me to depart." Blair exited the general store and her eyes locked with his.

Her brother was correct. Upon discovering his being well, she ought to return to Newark at once. However, as Blair climbed into the seat next to hers, he grinned at her and she smiled back, well aware of the fact that her desire to remain in the Mohawk Valley was not solely due to P.J.

*   *   *

Blair sank into his bed with a sigh of pleasure. After today's fight, a good night's sleep ought to help ease some of his weariness.

He closed his eyes and sank farther into his straw mattress. *Thank You, God, for not allowing worse harm to befall us.*

He rested his hands behind his head. He never thought Penny could shoot a pistol. A smile slid across his face. Amid all that expensive silk clothing lingered a woman he yearned to know more.

He sighed, then rolled over in an effort to help himself fall asleep faster, because ever since the first day he had met Penny, she had flitted into his dreams and made his nights a thing to look forward to.

"Nay!" Elsie's voice shrieked into the silent night air. "You mustn't do this!" her familiar wail made him jump out of bed. "Do you not love us?" He pulled his dressing gown on over his nightshirt and grabbed his candle, before he raced to her room, just as he'd done nearly every night since she'd come. And thus far, he'd been successful at reaching her before

Halcyon or Mickey clamored out of their room.

"Elsie, you need not fret." He swung her door open. "I'm here." He clamped his mouth shut. His feet grew roots into the wood floor. Penny sat in the rocking chair, hugging his niece, as she brushed away her tears.

Their eyes met over Elsie's head. She cradled his niece as if she were her mother. The sight took his breath.

"Hush now," Penny cooed. "'Twas only a bad dream."

"Nay," Elsie cried. "He was dreadfully mean," she sobbed into Penny's nightgown. Penny rubbed her back.

"Elsie." He placed his candle on her bedside table, then knelt beside the rocking chair. "'Twas the same dream?" She nodded. He laid his hand on her heaving back. "'Tis over now." With a yawn, she nodded and snuggled farther into her nanny's embrace.

He withdrew his hand. His fingers had been mere inches from Penny's. And yet, her warmth radiated straight to his heart. He remained motionless. His eyes fixed on the embrace. As Elsie settled back to sleep, he couldn't imagine a more loving woman.

Or a more beautiful one. His eyes roamed to her shoulders, where her golden locks lay loose. Had she been brushing her hair, unable to tuck her locks under her nightcap, when she heard his niece's cry? Elsie always insisted her hair be brushed one hundred times. His reverie vanished the moment Penny's eyes met his. How drab the ocean would appear in comparison.

"Is she asleep?" he whispered. Penny peered down. His gaze followed hers. Elsie's wee chest rose and fell in a slow rhythm. Their eyes met once more. She dipped her chin.

He stood, bent over the rocking chair, and lifted Elsie from her arms. Their limbs touched. He forced his thoughts onto his niece as she groaned and rolled into his chest.

He stilled to assure she remained asleep. Once she settled, he proceeded to her bed with slow, careful steps. Gently, he set her down. Before he straightened, his head whipped left.

Penny had slid along his side to pull blankets atop Elsie.

He grabbed his candle, intent on busying himself.

"Pray tell, what bad dream plagues her?" she whispered, peering down with compassion at the lass' sleeping form.

He jerked his head toward the door. They ought to converse in the corridor. She nodded. But a flush crept over her cheeks. Perhaps she had just realized she donned nothing more than her nightgown. With haste, she grabbed an extra blanket from the foot of Elsie's bed. With a fling of her slender arms, she draped the wool over her shoulders and pulled the material tight about her as if the blanket were a fashionable shawl. He couldn't take his eyes from her. Beautiful didn't even begin to describe her.

"Shall we?" she asked.

Abruptly, he turned and strode from the room. Fortunately, his feet knew where to lead, because his mind needed a moment to right itself. "We can observe Elsie from here." He motioned to a trunk. As she sat he laid the candle at their feet, then joined her. "I moved this here once I realized her bad dreams came nearly every night."

Although, on all those previous nights, he'd sat here alone, the darkness of night seeping desolation into his bones. He rubbed his hands down the length of his thighs. Having Penny beside him warmed him more than a roaring fire and chased those dark feelings away.

"Pray tell, what bad dream frequents her?" Her concerned eyes moved from Elsie to rest on him. "She declared that *he was quite mean*. Who is *he*?"

His hands fisted. "Her father."

She blew out a disconcerted breath. "I thought as much."

"Come morning, she shall refuse to speak of him, even deny the remembrance of her bad dream. However, some nights, she bellows or murmurs enough that I've deemed her father a monster."

Her eyes shot to the bedroom. "Oh, sweet lass." She shook her head.

"What compelled your sister to wed such a brute?" She faced him. "I apologize. Your sister may not deserve blame. I know there are those who are extremely apt at disguising themselves, and behave in such convincing ways that they truly fool even the smartest of us." She scratched her neck. She hadn't deceived Blair with malicious intentions. Still, a bitter taste settled in her mouth. "Could your sister not discern his wickedness before they wed? Did not you?"

He inhaled deeply. "I had not the privilege of meeting my sister until after she had married. By then, Elsie was well past her first birthday."

"Nay?" Her features crinkled. "How can that be?" His fingers raked through his hair. She bit her lower lip. "Once more, I apologize for my imprudence."

"Nay, please, you mustn't apologize." He leaned forward, his fingers fastened upon a fallen strand of her hair. He hadn't meant to touch her, but his knuckles brushed her cheek. Her skin was softer than he had ever imagined possible. He moved the tendril behind her shoulder. She faced him, her mouth slightly agape. "I trust you explicitly with my niece, am I correct to assume I can trust you with this, as well?"

Her wide eyes held his. "Most certainly, I shall keep your confidence."

He forced himself to inch backwards, away from her, until his back rested on the wall. "My mother harbored plenty of secrets from my father. She believed herself to be a good woman and merely devised lies, or omitted the truth, to avoid causing him pain or anger. According to her, she yearned to shield him."

With earnest interest, her blue eyes remained fixed on him. The tension in his neck eased. His mother's secrets were known to those in their circles, however, he'd never told the tale. And he'd never shared how her secrets had affected him.

"That day, six years ago, is now a permanent fixture in my mind. My parents and I were enjoying tea before the fire, as was our usual, but that day, a knock sounded on our door that altered our lives forevermore."

He peered into Elsie's bedroom, then slowly met Penny's gaze once more. How would she perceive him, and his family, after she heard their history? The urge to avoid the tale grew strong, but he wouldn't behave as his mother had. He didn't wish to form an attachment akin to his parents. If he and Penny were to ever procure a future together, he wished for their love to be grounded in honesty.

"My mother opened the door, as my father and I stepped into the vestibule. A woman, nearly a decade older than me, stood pensive, with a child propped on her hip."

"Elsie and your sister?" she asked.

He nodded. "She had been in search of my mother for years and blurted that she was her daughter. My father dropped his teacup. Their resemblance made her assertion undeniable."

She laid her hand atop his, her warm fingers curled with

companionship. A jolt shot through his chest. She wasn't repulsed.

"As you may imagine, a profusion of yelling and hysterics followed. My family nearly ripped apart when my mother confirmed that she had indeed born a child before she had met my father."

"I often wonder if my parents had been in a similar situation and that led them to abandon my brother and I." Her eyes rested on their joined hands.

"I wish you didn't suffer with these unanswered questions." He stroked her hand.

She shrugged. "I'm well aware of people's prejudices toward my brother and myself because of our parentage—or lack thereof, but we refuse to allow such pettiness to bother us. Instead, we declare ourselves thankful for being blessed with an unconditionally loving adopted family."

He smiled. "Anyone who holds you accountable for your parents' actions are not worth your aggravation."

She nodded. "Thank you. I do hope Elsie doesn't suffer."

"She's never mentioned being the object of such torment."

"Good. I hope that remains so." Her lips stretched into a slow smile.

"I do, as well. And people here know the details of my mother's life. She ceased to lie from that day forward. She simply laid bare all her secrets." He chuckled. "She even proclaimed her utter abhorrence of my father's beard and wished him to rid himself of his facial hair immediately."

She laughed. The sweet, tender sound hummed to his core. "Their marriage survived?"

"They strove to work past the lies. I cannot attest to its having been easy. It all but destroyed their marriage and nearly damaged my father beyond repair. I pray I'm never faced with such tribulations." He blew out a long, slow breath. "Trust is the most essential element in a marriage, do you not agree?"

She nodded.

Her understanding compelled him to explain further, "My mother wasn't an evil woman. She was left to fend for herself at a tender age. She kept herself from the poorhouse by accepting whatever work availed itself to her, be it as a scullery maid, laundress, housekeeper, or whatnot. However, the final house she worked in before she arrived here, was owned by a man who believed he owned his workers, as well. He took every liberty he wished, and that is how my sister came to be. My mother had been defenseless, a mere domestic servant, whilst he held a high standing in society. She was repeatedly raped, without anyone to aid her, or anywhere to flee."

Her hand covered her lips. Her eyes drooped with empathy. "And when she conceived?"

"He denied he had fathered the baby. He accused her of prostitution, and banished her from his house."

"Nay!" She shuddered under her makeshift shawl. "But, the child belonged to him. How did she survive?"

"She threw herself on the church's mercy, and a couple who couldn't bear children took her in.

After my sister was born she left her with them."

"I cannot imagine the anguish of leaving one's baby." Her eyes floated to Elsie. "I've been her nanny for only a short while and I already love her dearly."

He grinned. If the decision were his, she'd never leave his home. "She adores you, as well, Princess Penelope."

"Princess?" she grimaced. "Certainly, you cannot insist on referring to me as such?"

He shrugged. "Elsie's reasoning is sound. You are devoid of any knowledge of your lineage, and you are most assuredly the loveliest woman I've ever beheld."

Her lips parted.

He leaned in.

His arm rubbed her blanket, accidentally causing the edge to fall from her shoulder. He caught the mass of wool and pulled the material back over her snowy nightgown. She shivered under his touch. Her intense blue eyes widened.

He pulled the blanket under her
chin, his fingers very near to her
skin. He yearned to feel her full,
rosy lips under his.

She moved closer.

His heart hammered in his chest.

"Blair," her voice was
breathless.

His eyes flashed to hers, in wait
of her invitation, in hope of her
ardent declaration.

7

Penelope saw the longing in Blair's smoldering gaze. Her skin tingled with goose-flesh. She may be a novice in the affairs of the heart, but she understood Blair. He wished to embrace

her, and she was lost in the dark
flecks of his eyes.

Earlier, she hadn't known if he
was naught more than a brutal warden.
But here, she sat alongside a man who
had proven himself to be anything but
needlessly aggressive. She admired his
defense of her brother. And now, his
compassion for his niece melted her
insides. Blair McAllister was not an
ordinary man.

But she had never intended to
care for him. And yet, his
vulnerability enticed her. She ached
to alleviate his troubles and worries.

He leaned closer.

"Blair," she whispered his name
once more.

The air was heavy. The attraction
between them undeniable. She had felt
the strength of his allure from their
very first moment together, when the
dust had settled and she had locked
eyes with him, after he had put his
life at risk to save hers. He truly
was her hero.

But she wasn't worthy of him. Not
whilst she propagated lies. Sure, she
had never uttered an outright

falsehood, but she neglected to be honest about her relationship to Paul. That was unfair to him.

He professed that a marriage required trust. Certainly, trust depended on honesty—something she couldn't offer, especially with the uncertainty of his reaction to the truth. If her brother was harmed because of her foolish actions she would never be able to live with herself.

"We ought to return to our rooms." She stood. "Elsie's has quieted and isn't stirring."

He took a deep breath. "I suppose you're correct." He leaned down to retrieve his candle before he rose as slow as the sun. "Although I pray my niece never suffers from another bad dream, I enjoyed our discussion, and do hope the chance presents itself again."

"I enjoyed our conversation, as well." She wrapped her arms around her blanket tighter. But as much as she relished being with him, wishing to share an intimate kiss as much as he had, she couldn't permit such closeness again. Being honest with him was out of the question, and beginning an attachment with anything less, would only end in suffering. She couldn't hurt him. She wouldn't. He was a good man. He deserved better. "Goodnight, Blair."

*   *   *

Blair secured the lock to the door that housed his prisoners of war. Such measures were hardly necessary to imprison Paul, but they were imperative for Clyde. Truly he ought to speak with his superiors to separate them. Paul ought to enjoy better treatment. Forcing Paul to live under the same restrictive parole agreement as Clyde was unfair. The two men stood in stark contrast to one another. But, that matter must wait for another day. He swung his keys and stepped out from the shelter of the forest to behold the setting sun turning orange.

"Blair," Lachlan McAllister called from across the field after leaving his horse in Mickey's expert care.

He waved at his cousin. His visit was unexpected. Usually Lachlan spent his evenings with his betrothed, Fiona Robertson. "Is something amiss?" He studied his cousin's face and the sling that supported the shoulder wound he had obtained as an officer in this war.

"Nay." Lachlan grinned and clapped him on the back. "All is fine. I've come on business."

"Shall we discuss it over tea and biscuits? I was about to retire for the night."

"A fine suggestion." Lachlan fell into step beside him.

"Are you prepared for your wedding?" he asked.

"More than ready. I've wanted to marry Fiona for as long as I can remember, and finally the day is nearly upon us. Saturday cannot arrive soon enough. I've even developed a habit of staring at the clock. And trust me, the minutes pass extremely slowly." Shaking his head, he pulled out his pocket watch. "Tick, tick,

tick, see how they taunt a man hopelessly in love," he laughed, then stowed his metal timepiece. "Any progress learning more about that woman you saved?"

A silly grin must have crept over his face, because his cousin's eyebrow arched in amusement. "I've hired her as Elsie's nanny."

"Then I gather you've discovered more than merely her name."

"Actually, I hoped to invite her to your wedding."

"As Elsie's nanny or your companion?"

"If the decision lay entirely with me, the latter. But unfortunately, I'm unsure of her feelings. Perhaps when I invite her to the wedding I shall be able to garner some wisdom." Because when they had talked last night he thought she had harbored similar feelings, but then she had abruptly stood and announced they ought to return to their bedchambers, and he was left more than confused.

"Better make haste." Lachlan pulled out his pocket watch once more.

"Only thirty-eight hours and forty-five minutes until my wedding," he beamed, and Blair chuckled as they entered through the front entrance door.

"Lachlan!" Elsie ran down the corridor.

"Mind his shoulder," Blair warned as Elsie embraced him.

"May I play with your sling once your shoulder heals?" she asked, eyeing the material.

"You may have it." Lachlan tweaked her nose as Penny approached.

"Penny, this is my cousin, Lachlan McAllister," he introduced her, purposely ignoring the teasing look his cousin shot at him.

"Pleased to make your acquaintance." Lachlan extended his hand.

"And Lachlan, this is Miss Penelope Sherwood," he continued.

"Your name." Lachlan looked quizzically between him and Penny. "It sounds familiar."

"Perhaps whilst Penny resided at Pastor West's?" he suggested. "She travelled down to the Mohawk Valley

from Upper Canada to swap homes with
the pastor's daughter. But, ever since
she became Elsie's nanny, she's been
living here." He glanced at her. He
hoped she'd remain here indefinitely.

"Penelope Sherwood, from Upper
Canada?" Lachlan glared at her.

She nodded. Then her eyes grew
large, as if she had just remembered
him. "Your betrothed is Fiona
Robertson, correct?"

"Aye," he replied tersely, and
the tension that erupted thickened
like a storm cloud. What had happened?

"Ladies, I do apologize, but
Lachlan has come on business and we
must address it promptly." He had to
do something to diffuse the situation.
"Would you mind asking Halcyon to send
us tea and biscuits?"

Penny nodded and took hold of his
niece's shoulders. "'Twas nice to meet
you, Lachlan."

Lachlan barely dipped his chin in
response. "Goodnight, Elsie," he
managed to utter before he stalked
into Blair's study.

"I shall be in to say goodnight
when I'm finished." He kissed Elsie's

forehead. Straightening to his full height, his eyes met Penny's. He drew his lips into a smile then followed Lachlan into his study and closed the door.

"She's Elsie's nanny?" Lachlan raged. "The woman you're smitten with?"

"Aye." He crossed his arms. "Why should that upset you?"

"Because—" he pointed at the door "—that woman helped Jamilyn in her attempt to separate me from the love of my life."

Blair grabbed the back of a chair and gripped the upholstery tight. His knuckles whitened, as the memory of what Lachlan and Fiona had suffered at the hands of the pastor's daughter and her informant from Upper Canada rushed back to him. "Surely, you're mistaken?"

As he began to pace, Lachlan shook his head. "I remember her name clearly. How could I not? She was vital to Jamilyn's disastrous plan to claim me for herself. Penelope was the one who fed Jamilyn the information from Upper Canada that she used to drive Fiona out of town." His face rumpled in disgust.

"Are you certain Penny helped Jamilyn?"

"You read the letter Fiona wrote me the day she fled. She had been the victim of defamation in Upper Canada, and Penelope, Jamilyn's friend from Newark informed her about those rumors, perhaps she even had a hand in them. I cannot fathom why Penelope hated Fiona enough to enable Jamilyn to spread those lies here."

"But thankfully, Jamilyn didn't succeed in spreading any misinformation."

"Aye, but she did frighten Fiona into leaving me." Lachlan's hands balled into fists.

"I remember." He stopped strangling the chair and dropped into the cushioned seat. "But I've come to know, Penny. She's a caring woman. I cannot believe her capable of such hurtful behaviour."

"You've only known her for a mere matter of days. She may not be who she seems." He silenced himself when a knock sounded on the door. Blair welcomed Halcyon in with their refreshments.

"Take heed, Penelope is friends with Jamilyn," Lachlan continued once Halcyon quit the room. "I wouldn't underestimate what she's capable of."

Blair exhaled a deep breath. He couldn't deny their friendship. After all, she had swapped houses with the pastor's daughter. But they were friends who resided in separate countries. Surely, they weren't as close as black on a kettle.

"I do apologize." Lachlan sank into the chair opposite him. "You finally found a nanny for Elsie, not to mention being smitten for the first time, and this is the news you're handed." He shook his head. "How I wish things could have ended differently." He tore into a biscuit.

"You sound as if the matter is settled." Blair eyed him over his teacup. "This is far from over." He blew at the steam. "Penny deserves a chance to explain herself."

"Fine. Question her." He waved a piece of his biscuit at him. "But don't allow love to blind you."

"I shan't." He drank his tea. God would help him discern the truth.

Lachlan popped the morsel into his mouth. "Good, because you deserve better."

"Thank you," he smirked at his cousin. "But I wish you would cease lamenting. Jamilyn didn't succeed in her plans. She's in Upper Canada, and unbeknownst to her, Pastor West sent Cole to watch over her. So don't fear her returning in an attempt to ruin your wedding."

Lachlan narrowed his eyes. "Is that the purpose of Penelope's presence? Was she sent by Jamilyn?"

He took a deep breath. "Let me ease your concern, I shall keep a close eye on her."

"Thank you." Lachlan stirred his tea. "I continue to pray Jamilyn has changed her ways, and now, I suppose I must likewise pray I'm mistaken about Penelope."

He drank his tea. He would pray for that, as well. "Now, to what do I actually owe the honor of your visit?"

He sighed, then smiled, obviously he found changing the subject just as difficult as Blair. "I've received orders that your prisoners are to be sent south."

"Oh?" He replaced his teacup into its saucer.

"Aye, Clyde has been deemed too great of a flee risk to live this close to the border."

He nodded. "It's unfortunate though that Paul must be lumped in with him. He's a good man."

"Perhaps you could send a note to the next warden." Lachlan settled back into his chair.

"I do wish to ensure Paul is treated less harshly. I shall certainly speak with this new warden when I meet him."

Lachlan shook his head. "I arranged for someone to arrive on Monday morning to take them south. I thought to save you from having to leave Elsie."

"How thoughtful, thank you. I appreciate your concern. The poor lass is still much affected, and suffers from bad dreams."

"I gathered as much, and I'm sorry." Lachlan frowned. "How is Cindy faring?"

He pursed his lips. "There has yet to be a change. She continues to sit in that cabin staring at her hands during the day and then sleeps prolonged hours at night. However, she doesn't fight Halcyon when she feeds or bathes her, which is a blessing. But she doesn't look anyone in the eye. 'Tis as if her body is here, but she is not."

"Has the doctor been to see her lately?"

"Aye, and he maintains she may never respond to anyone ever again. He refuses to utter any false hope on the matter."

"I'm sorry. I shall continue to pray she recovers."

Blair dipped his chin. "Thank you. Her condition is entirely in God's hands."

*   *   *

After Lachlan departed, Blair closed the door and leaned his forehead against the wood. Suppose Lachlan's suspicions were true? Jamilyn could have easily discovered his want of a nanny, given that her father was the one commissioned to find a suitable one. She could have, in all possibility, have sent Penny here to cause trouble.

He squeezed his eyes closed. Penny *had* shown an over eagerness to become Elsie's nanny. Was she here to execute Jamilyn's plan to keep Fiona from marrying Lachlan?

He turned and let his eyes wander toward the stairs that led to Penny's whereabouts. He detested his thoughts. She had shown nothing but care and kindness to both him and Elsie. Even last night, her tender side had emerged. She'd bared her emotions whilst she had spoken of her past.

Then again, she had abruptly ended that discussion. Had she turned away because somehow falling in love would ruin her plan?

He shook his head and stepped forward. He may ponder this until daybreak, but he shan't arrive at any conclusions. To solve this, he must confront her.

Penelope backed quietly out of Elsie's bedroom. That adorable little lass had labored rather hard to stay awake waiting for Blair, but her heavy eyelids ultimately won. With a sigh she uttered a prayer that to-night Elsie would enjoy a peaceful sleep.

"Penny." Blair's voice sent her hand rushing to her heart. "I apologize," he whispered at the sight of her surprise.

She smiled and waved away his apology. "Despite herself, Elsie just fell asleep."

"I'm sorry for my prolonged delay."

She dipped her chin. "I explained to Elsie that your discussion with Lachlan must have been important, and she understood," she rambled, once she had noticed something in his countenance she had never seen before. Something was undoubtedly amiss.

"I must speak with you," his tone was even, completely unlike his usual friendly disposition.

She nodded. She couldn't very well refuse him. "Is something troubling you?" She adjusted her skirt as she sat on the trunk. He combed his fingers through his hair and looked anywhere but in her direction. She braced herself. Her back straightened as if a plank of wood pressed her spine into place. "Blair?"

Swimming with unease, his eyes met hers. "I know your secret."

She gasped. *He knew her secret?*

Her heart raced. Devoid of control, the chambers clamored wilder than that wagon that had nearly killed her. Her mind heaved to the conclusion that he ought not to have saved her, because now, his good deed had allowed her to place her brother's life in jeopardy.

She panted for breath. Her head dizzy. How would he punish them? Her brother had insisted she leave at once. He had warned her that her presence here was exceedingly dangerous.

"Penny," he repeated. Her neck snapped in his direction. "Did you not think I would discover the true reason for your travels? You do hail from Upper Canada."

"Then, you know?" her voice squeaked.

His eyes bored into hers. "Aye." A frown etched his face.

"I'm sorry." She turned. Her whole body now faced him. "You must understand, I wished to tell you, truly I did. But somehow—" she looked down and fumbled with her dress "—I simply couldn't." Tears stung her eyes. "You're a warden."

"You were afraid? Of me?" his voice hitched, as if the thought of her being frightened of him wounded him deeply.

The gentlest touch brought her chin up. Once more, she gazed into the depths of his brown eyes. Only now, the hardness had faded. "You needn't be scared of me."

"How could I not be? As a warden you possess the means and the power to punish. I was, I still am, completely at your mercy. How was I to know how you would react? The risk was too great."

"Penny," he sighed. "I expect the truth." She nodded, and rubbed her hands together. "You must have discerned how much trust means to me? My mother's lies nearly tore my family apart. Dishonesty is the worst poison."

"Aye." She couldn't meet his eyes as she mumbled, "That's why, last night, I drew away from you. I couldn't allow our attachment to progress further whilst I knew I had failed to be completely honest with you."

His eyebrows shot up. "Had this secret not gnawed on your conscience you would have returned my feelings?"

She stared at him. "Regrettably, that's irrelevant now," she gulped, and a shiver ran up her spine. His expression held an intensity that revealed that on the contrary he thought it did indeed still matter. "But," she sputtered. "You know I kept a secret. How shall you ever be able to trust me now?"

He studied her, not answering for a long while, "Tell me why. Tell me everything. Then perhaps we can move past this."

She nodded. Hope soared through her. She had lived in such dread since she had arrived. And now, thinking she could finally be free of it, filled her with a happiness she had never imagined possible. *Thank You, God, for making Blair such a benevolent man.*

"I know not where to begin," she couldn't keep the elation out of her voice. She wanted to unburden herself. And his encouragement made her believe that if she divulged everything, he would understand. He already knew her secret. He just wished to hear the words from her.

If only she had known earlier that he wouldn't accuse her of trying to help her brother escape. She never would have had to hide anything.

She smiled at how incredibly blessed she felt knowing that he believed they could get past this. *Please, God, let us have a future together.*

8

"**P**erhaps you ought to start at the beginning, Penny." Blair leaned farther back and crossed his arms. "Start with why you purposely spread false rumors about Fiona's unwarranted reputation in Upper Canada."

Penelope's jaw dropped open. "What?" Her mind battled for understanding.

"Are you denying that you were Jamilyn's informant from Upper Canada?" He sat up rigid, his eyes narrowed.

She blinked several times. What was happening? This entire conversation hadn't been centered on the fact that P.J. was her brother? He didn't know her secret after all?

She stood. "I need a drink of water." But what she truly needed, was a moment to come to terms with what had just transpired.

"Fine." He rose. "I shall fetch you a glass."

"Nay," she squeezed her eyes shut as she answered. She couldn't have him do things for her. "I shall retrieve the water myself. Would you care for some?"

He shook his head. "Nay, but let's both go. We can discuss this in my study. I don't wish to wake Elsie. And if she suffers one of her bad dreams, my study's close enough, considering we'd be able to hear her scream from the barn."

She nodded, then followed him down the stairs. She trembled to think how close she had actually come to revealing her secret.

Stumbling on a stair, she righted herself as he glanced over his shoulder. He must sense her unease, only he thought her agitation due to some secret regarding Fiona.

She stared at his back. Her situation had gone from dismal to dire. She had confirmed his suspicion that she had indeed kept a secret. In fact, she had sounded happy to discuss the matter with him. Now her only course of action was to keep up this fallacy or he might suspect she did indeed harbor another secret—and she couldn't allow that to happen.

She hugged herself as she trailed him into the kitchen. "You may wait in my study, Penny. I shan't be but a moment with your water." He turned and she stepped back to avoid contact with him.

With pierced lips she nodded, then spun on her heel and left the room. She had to keep her wits about her or this was not going to end well.

She slumped onto a chair in his study, rubbed her brow, then shook her head. How had this happened? She took a deep breath and opened her eyes. It mattered not. The only thing that did, was getting out of here alive.

Her brother had been correct—she shouldn't be here. This was far too dangerous. If she survived this conversation, she'd leave as soon as possible. She'd keep a constant prayer vigil for Elsie and of course stay in touch with her through letters. But—she fought back tears—she would miss Elsie.

And she couldn't lie to herself. Her eyes sought Blair the moment he entered the room. She would miss him immensely.

"Your water." He held a glass out to her.

"Thank you." She took the water and fiddled with the glass as he sat opposite her in an identical chair.

"It seems I'm destined to spend my evening in this room."

Did he wish to lighten the mood? She didn't respond. She merely peered into her clear liquid. If only sipping this purity would wash away the muddy water she had to wade through.

"Blair, I understand why you think I purposely spread false rumors about Fiona." She dared to meet his gaze. "Because you're correct, I was Jamilyn's informant from Upper Canada."

He grimaced. But underneath, she thought she saw how her words wounded him—at least she hoped her assessment of his feelings were accurate. "It was never my intention to harm Fiona," she attempted to eradicate his unease.

"Then why did you tell Jamilyn about the rumors?"

She leaned forward. Her fingers squeezed her drinking vessel. If she were stronger the glass would have shattered. "Jamilyn wrote to me about a woman from Queenston who had come here by the name of Fiona Robertson. She asked me if I knew Fiona, and if I did, what exactly I knew about her."

After taking a deep breath, she
continued, "I responded that I did
indeed know Fiona, but we were never
bosom friends. Fiona lived on the
other side of Queenston, too far for
us to have had much interaction. And
after her aunt and uncle died she
spent the entirety of her time running
their homestead alone."

She took a breath, then rushed
on, "But her deceased aunt had been
friends with my mother, and hence, we
were quite glad Fiona had come here.
There were indeed terrible rumors
about her that were being spread
throughout Upper Canada. Rumors
regarding her virtue—" she dropped
her voice "—but my family and I never
believed them. And not once did I
fathom Jamilyn would repeat what I had
told her in confidence, let alone use
my knowledge to cause injury to
Fiona."

She sat back to distance herself
from his glare. She had spoken the
truth and yet he looked entirely
unconvinced. Hence, her lips rambled
uncontrollably, "Jamilyn and I have
been friends since our first meeting

when we were adolescents. 'Twas of
course after I had been adopted when
Jamilyn's uncle brought her to Upper
Canada to conduct business with my pa.
But, since then, we've only been in
each other's company a few times. We
wrote letters on a regular basis, and
I thought I knew Jamilyn well enough,
but obviously not sufficiently enough,
considering I never once guessed how
she had planned to use my information
in such an abominable way."

"So you were unaware that Jamilyn
maliciously planned to use those
rumors against Fiona, to force Fiona
to leave Lachlan?" He crossed his
arms, his tone critical, as if he were
certain he had just caught her in a
web of deceit.

"Again, at the time I divulged
the information, I didn't possess even
an inkling of suspicion toward her
behavior. However, once she had been
caught and realized she had lost
Lachlan to Fiona forever, Jamilyn
exposed her misdeeds to me." She
paused in an attempt to discern
whether he believed her. But such a

tactic proved futile, he sat as still as a statue with unreadable emotions.

"You may not be aware of this, Blair, but Jamilyn is sorry. That's the reason she insisted we swap homes. She wished to distance herself from this town, and everything that transpired here, so she could set herself right."

She played with a strand of her hair. "According to Jamilyn, she's in Upper Canada as an act of penance." She tucked the strand behind her ear and sat up straighter. "You must understand, she's ashamed. Hence why, she poured her heart out to me and told me of everything she had done. She knows her actions and thoughts were wrong. And she profusely apologized to me for undermining what I had told her in confidence. She's asked my forgiveness—"

"She should have asked for Lachlan and Fiona's forgiveness, as well."

"I believe she shall. But she requires some time, and distance, first. She's an intelligent woman. She knows she needs to set her mind right.

And Lachlan and Fiona need time before they shall be able to accept her apology." She sipped her water, but he still sat with every one of his muscles utterly rigid.

"I want to believe you." His eyes remained glued to hers.

"Then please do believe me about this, because I speak the truth." His expression didn't alter. She sucked in a long breath. She must think of another way to convince him. She could send a letter to Jamilyn and have her write to Blair, but how long would such a correspondence take? Too long. She wasn't staying. And besides, he may not even believe Jamilyn. "Blair, can you arrange for me to visit Fiona?"

His eyes widened. "I'm not certain she'd welcome your visit. She may be extremely hostile toward you."

"I understand." She pursed her lips. "I'm fully aware of the battle Lachlan fought to remain civil with me, but I must try. I must apologize for my role in this and offer an explanation. Perhaps I may be able to mend things between Jamilyn and Fiona and Lachlan. I would be most pleased to know that when she returns she shall come home to people willing to accept her apology." She leaned forward and candidly met the intensity of his eyes. "Furthermore, I dearly wish to prove my innocence to you."

He stared back at her for a long moment. She fought the urge to fidget under his scrutiny, especially when he leaned forward and lessened the gap between them. "You need not prove anything to me."

Surely her heart had just stopped. His words enthralled her like a snake charmer. She sputtered, "I realize you weren't directly hurt by the information I supplied Jamilyn, but I've come to consider us as friends—" more than friends actually, but she kept that part to herself "—and I sincerely wish that you do indeed know I would never intentionally hurt anyone."

He reached for her hand, his warmth raced through her fingers, up her arm, and straight into the center of her chest. "You misunderstood me, Penny. You need not prove a thing to

me, because I already believe you." He
believed her? *Thank You, God.* "And I'm
truly sorry Jamilyn placed you in such
a precarious situation."

She squeezed his hand, not
trusting her voice, because although
she felt gratitude, love coursed
through her veins.

"I shall take you to visit Fiona
and Lachlan to-morrow." She nodded. "I
do wish for this to be resolved
posthaste so we may all move forward."

She gulped. She wanted nothing
more than to move forward with him.
Unfortunately, she knew that was
impossible.

*　　*　　*

As Blair toiled through his
workday, his mind constantly wandered
to thoughts of Penny. He believed in
her innocence, but his unease
heightened as the hours climbed.
Suppose Fiona and Lachlan didn't
believe her story or accept her
apology? Their visit could dovetail
into disaster and he'd be caught in

the middle. He turned his eyes toward the summer sky. He needed God's help.

After he locked Paul and Clyde into their cabin for the night, he prayed, as he forced his feet to trudge home. But his footsteps stalled when he saw Penny standing a foot or so outside the front door. She was beautiful. And straightaway, his mind flung itself into questions about what his life would be like to be married to her and come home to her every night. A smile spread across his lips and he put his hand up in greeting.

She waved back and he watched the breeze flap along her cream-colored, empire waist gown. As he neared her, the petit red roses that covered the flowing calico material sprung to life. Such delicate flowers made her appear even more gentle and feminine. And looking at her, 'twas impossible to conceive of anyone believing her capable of malice. She was the picture of sweetness.

"Do you still wish to visit Fiona and Lachlan?" he asked, his stomach sick at the thought of her being berated.

"Aye," she answered without hesitation. "If I somehow hurt Fiona and Lachlan, I must apologize and make amends."

He dipped his chin. "Is Elsie prepared to set off?"

"She shall be with us in a moment," she smiled, laughter in her eyes. "She's on a mission to beg Halcyon to wrap up some table scraps for Lachlan and Fiona's dogs."

He chuckled, "She certainly adores those animals."

"Indeed, and I do believe after all the stories and descriptions I've heard to-day, I know them better than anyone, with the exception of Elsie herself of course."

He dipped his chin, then turned to face the wagon Mickey had prepared for them. "Shall we seat you whilst we wait?"

"I cannot think of any reason not to." She stepped forward lightly. Then, her jovial mood faded. "But, Blair—" her blue eyes held his "—I need to speak with you regarding my employment here."

"Oh?" His eyebrows slammed together. "Is something amiss?" He searched her face.

She hesitated. And with each second that passed his muscles clenched tighter. "I couldn't conceive of a better way to broach this subject." As her face grew more solemn, his stomach flipped violently. "But I suppose, I'm perpetually at a loss as to where to begin when I attempt to tell you something of importance." Her lips rose in the corners a wee bit, but he couldn't return her smile. The gravity in her voice, and the severity in her blue eyes, told him he wouldn't welcome the words she was about to utter.

"I've secured the food." Elsie ran to them.

"Wonderful." Penny found her voice before he could and ripped her eyes from his to watch Elsie hold her satchel up with pride. "I'm certain the dogs shall love you all the more for this." Penny patted his niece's hair.

"Uncle Blair, you look ill."
Elsie took his hand and his attention
away from Penny.

"I'm fine," his voice scratched
more gruffly than usual, but he
managed to smile down at her. "Allow
me to help you into the wagon." He
strode toward the side and lifted
Elsie in. Sensing Penny's approach, he
turned and offered her his hand. "We
shall speak about your matter once we
find ourselves alone once more," he
spoke the words because he had to, not
because he wished to. And the look of
concern that glimmered in her blue
eyes reconfirmed that this was one
conversation he didn't wish to partake
in.

"Of course." She nodded, as she
took his hand and seated herself.
"Thank you." She withdrew her fingers.
As he plodded to his side of the
wagon, he rubbed his palms down the
front of his shirt. He had to do
something to take away the chill that
had pervaded his skin.

Whilst he pulled himself up into
the seat, he marveled at how her
beauty intensified when she smiled.

Elsie must have said something to cause her mirth, however her happiness failed to last, and soon she grew solemn as he commanded his horses to set off.

Elsie chattered incessantly the entire ride, but like him, Penny merely nodded or emitted short responses as she watched the passing land. She was certainly deep in thought and the mystery of what entertained her mind stabbed at him. He stole a glance at her. And his hands tightened on the reins once he realized she may well be nervous to speak with Fiona and Lachlan. Perhaps she had concluded that if they didn't accept her, he'd dismiss her from his employment.

He glanced at her once more. She wrung her hands and a pang of compassion overtook him. The urge to take her hands and make her stop rubbing them was strong, but he fought it. His muscles flexed though, he shan't allow any harm to befall her.

He pulled his horses to a stop. "We've arrived." Elsie jumped down from the wagon and ran toward the house without waiting for them. "She's become quite attached to Lachlan and Fiona since she's come to live with me."

"It definitely appears so," Penny laughed as she waited for him to come around and help her down.

"Fiona's been residing in this house alone, whilst Lachlan lives with his parents, until they wed," he informed her, as they began to walk toward the house.

"It's charming." Her head swung around. "They're certain to be quite happy here."

He nodded, then blurted, "Would you be?" He remembered the fine silk gown she had worn on that first day when she had arrived in town, and wondered at the sort of life she imagined for herself, because 'twas clearly evident her parents were wealthy.

"I believe I would be." She didn't meet his eyes. "This house and this land would suit any couple, as long as they had the most important aspect of their marriage covered."

"And what pray tell is that?" He watched her, forcing himself not to respond to his feelings after her arm brushed against his.

"Love," she spoke just above a whisper, her eyes still diverted out into the distance.

His heart ached for her to look at him. And not just at this moment, but one day, soon, with the kind of love in her eyes that a wife reserved for her husband.

"Blair, regarding what we had begun to speak of earlier—" she stopped walking "—I know this is most definitely not the ideal time to unburden myself, but I must. I cannot keep this to myself a moment longer." Her blue eyes finally met his, but he didn't see in them what he had wished. "I do fully apologize from the depths of my heart, but I must resign as Elsie's nanny. I must return home."

*B*lair fumbled backwards as if someone had punched him in the stomach and knocked the air from his lungs. "Why must you return home, Penny?" the words escaped his lips, and yet, 'twas

completely incomprehensible that he
had actually uttered them. She was to
leave?

"I must go—for many different
reasons." She folded her arms over her
middle, and her fingers rubbed her
arms as if she needed to soothe
herself. But, if she didn't wish to
leave, then why had she ever made such
an outlandish suggestion.

"I was under the assumption you
would remain until the end of the
war?"

"And how many more years might
that be?"

He shrugged. "But you're safe
here." His head spun at the thought of
her living in Upper Canada whilst war
raged around her. His cousin, Cole,
had followed Jamilyn there to protect
her, but he couldn't leave Elsie to
follow Penny there, and he'd never
risk taking Elsie into a war zone.

"I shall be safe in Newark."

"You cannot guarantee that." His
fingers raked through his hair. "Have
I caused this desire to leave? I
apologize if any of my actions have

rendered you uncomfortable or angered—"

"Nay." Her right hand shot across the distance between them and landed on his forearm. "'Tis not because of you. I simply cannot alter my circumstances," her voice trailed off and she withdrew her hand.

"Please, explain your reasoning."

"I'm sorry." Her eyes filled with sadness. "I shall apologize to Lachlan and Fiona, but I cannot remain in a town where people believe me to be a malicious gossip."

"After you speak with them, I'm certain that shall be altered." She grimaced with doubt, so he took both of her arms in his hands. "They shall believe you, just as I do."

"But other reasons exist, as well." He studied her. His eyes pleaded with her to confide in him. However, she examined the dirt underfoot. "I do apologize, Blair, but my reasons are of a personal nature and I cannot explain them. Although, someday I do hope to."

He stepped in closer to her and lowered his voice, "Pray tell, how can I convince you to stay?"

Her blue eyes rose to meet his and brought with them a wave of emotion that crashed against his shaky shore. He searched against the tide, but her gaze held firm. "I fear you cannot. I've already spoken with Pastor West and he's assured me he shall find my replacement, someone equally suitable, that Elsie shan't only accept as her nanny, but adore."

Except, she shan't be you. He bit the inside of his cheek so his thoughts wouldn't spill forth.

"Uncle Blair." Elsie's voice caused him to drop Penny's arms.

"Are Fiona and Lachlan in the house?" he managed to ask after his niece had run to them.

"Fiona's in the kitchen, but Lachlan's feeding the horses." She took turns stroking two farm collie dogs that had run alongside her. "May I help, Lachlan?"

"Of course," he answered, unable to remove his eyes from Penny.

"Thank you," she called over her shoulder.

"I shall miss her dearly." Penny watched Elsie run to the stable.

"And she shall most definitely miss you terribly." He stepped in closer to her once more. Unwilling to even think of how much pain he'd endure. But he couldn't deny the facts any longer. Her wish to leave was a blatantly obvious sign that she didn't harbor the same feelings for him as he did for her. His chest constricted.

"Shall we?" She took a deep breath, then leaned back on her heels, before she turned to glance at Fiona's house.

He may not possess any thoughts besides her imminent departure, but her nerves were clearly visible. And he could not withstand the pain of witnessing her fret a moment longer. "That is why we came." He led her to the house. "Fiona," he called as he knocked on the open door.

They were already past the threshold when Fiona responded in a lively voice, "I'm in the kitchen."

He glanced at Penny before they walked into the room. "Sorry for this unannounced visit, Fiona, but I've brought a guest, someone you know from Upper Canada," he doubted he had succeeded in hiding the tension in his voice.

Fiona froze, her hands encased in the dough she had been kneading. "Penelope," the name stuck in her throat.

"Fiona." Penny stepped forward. "'Tis a pleasure to see you."

She wiped her hands on her apron. "And you, as well." Her eyes hit him with accusation as to why he had ever considered bringing Penny here.

Penny looked between him and Fiona, her hands together again as she scraped off a layer of skin. "I apologize if we've interrupted you," she spoke rapidly. The stiffness in the room was palpable, and he prayed she could eradicate it. "Your home is lovely."

"Thank you." Fiona glanced around the kitchen. "Before my parents died and I was sent to live with my aunt in Queenston, this was my family's home.

I hadn't been here since I was a wee lass," she spoke as hastily as Penny had. He, on the other hand, remained quiet. "Lachlan purchased the homestead for us from Blair."

"How very chivalrous of him, and most generous of you to let the property go, Blair." She locked her hands behind her back. "You're a most fortunate woman."

Fiona dipped her chin.

With a look toward him that clearly indicated this was the moment of reckoning, Penny took another deep breath then began, "The sole purpose of my visit is to apologize. I'm fully aware that my correspondence with Jamilyn included information about you. However, my intention was never to hurt you. I was completely unaware of her cruel intentions. I merely reiterated the events that had occurred in Upper Canada. Nevertheless, I'm deeply sorry. Jamilyn has apologized to me for breaking my trust and sharing the contents of my letter. And I know she regrets her actions and is sorry for attempting to thwart your relationship with Lachlan. And even though you possess every right to be angry with her, and me, 'tis my hope that when Jamilyn eventually returns she shall apologize and you shall be able to make amends."

Fiona didn't offer a response, she simply stared at her. In a hurry, Penny continued full of earnest, "My mother and your aunt were dear friends, and to hear your good name slandered throughout Upper Canada pained us. Please believe me, we never once supposed the allegations true and we argued with anyone who would listen, and many who refused. As I told Jamilyn, we were most happy to hear of your coming here and leaving such an absurdly erroneous reputation behind you in Upper Canada."

He flinched when Fiona stepped forward. Most assuredly he would aid Penny in her explanation if Fiona rejected her account, but for now he must ensure Fiona didn't slap her across the face.

"Thank you." Fiona took her hands, and he closed his eyes to thank God. "I don't hold you responsible for

Jamilyn's actions." She smiled at her. "My aunt loved your mother dearly, and because of that, I could never believe you'd intend to cause me pain."

"Indeed, I didn't. I never would." Penny still lacked a smile, but the knowledge that Fiona didn't despise her reassured him she'd soon alter that.

"If you shall excuse me, I wish to greet my cousin and see how Elsie is faring." He took a step back.

"You need not leave," Fiona told him.

He dipped his chin, as he lengthened the distance between them. "I do wish to discuss certain matters with Lachlan." *Such as Penny's innocence.*

"'Tis just as well—" Fiona drew Penny into her side "—we do indeed have much to discuss to reacquaint ourselves."

"We certainly do." And there it was, Penny's smile. Beautiful.

"Enjoy yourselves." He left with a smile of his own.

*　　*　　*

198

"Are men welcome in the kitchen?" Penelope heard Blair's familiar baritone as he entered the house.

"You most certainly are." Fiona gave her a knowing look as her cheerful voice danced down the hall. She averted her gaze, although she doubted that hid her blush. "Perhaps you could assist me in persuading Penelope to remain in the Mohawk Valley? I would dearly love to have a familiar face here, permanently."

He leaned against the doorjamb. "I assure you, that request is my top priority." His eyes locked with Penelope's. Her heart fluttered. She forced herself to look away, but she suspected she had allowed her eyes to linger far too long. Fiona's grin confirmed her suspicion. And her blush deepened at the look Fiona shot Blair. If only she could allow him to convince her to stay. But that wasn't possible. She must leave before anyone discerned that P.J. was her brother.

"Fiona, I cannot thank you enough for your understanding and hospitality."

"You're welcome." Fiona hugged her before they left.

"Elsie's still with Lachlan in the stable." Blair closed the door behind them. "I thought it best not to interrupt her fun until you were prepared to leave."

"How considerate." She looked up at him. "I shall walk with you to the stable." She fell into step with him.

"I'd like that." His serious brown orbs met hers. "Because if you shall permit me, I do have a question for you."

"By all means, ask me," she gulped out her response.

"Now that your friendship with Fiona has been restored, you should know I've spoken with Lachlan and assured him of Fiona's assessment of you, and he shall cease to hold you accountable for Jamilyn's actions as well."

"Thank you. 'Tis a relief." Her lips tipped upward. "However, 'twas not a question."

"Nay, 'twas not," he laughed, and gently took hold of her arm which slowed her feet to a stop. "I understand your desire to return home, but you must permit me the opportunity to alter your decision." He dropped his hand as she began to protest, but he continued, "Can you not remain here one additional day, because I'd be honored if you'd accompany me to Lachlan and Fiona's wedding tomorrow."

Her mouth gaped open. She hadn't expected such an invitation. "You mustn't attempt to change my mind," she fumbled out her words.

His hopeful expression fell.

"I'm sorry." She reached for his forearm. "'Tis not my intention to cause you pain." She bit her bottom lip and looked up into sad eyes. "Provided you accept that I shall depart after the wedding, then aye, I shall stay to attend the wedding with you."

He dipped his chin. But the spark she had often seen dance in his eyes was lost. He glanced down at her hand upon him before he quietly said, "I accept your wish to leave, but I refuse to abandon my prayers that you shall change your mind." His intensity overwhelmed her and her gaze fled to where her hand rested on his forearm.

Allowing herself to become attached to him would never do, she jerked her hand away and crossed her arms. She ought to have never agreed. What had possessed her? She didn't need this entanglement. If she left straightaway, she'd escape without anyone knowing P.J. was her brother—because not even Fiona knew of their kinship.

She had just probed Fiona with several covert questions, and thankfully Fiona's years spent as a hermit on her homestead in Queenston, coupled with P.J.'s frequent and long stretches of absence from Upper Canada, had caused her to forget Penelope even had a brother. She was now quite grateful that in their earlier years P.J. had been sent to attend school in Britain. In those years, she had missed him dreadfully, but now, what a blessing in disguise the separation had been. Fiona wouldn't recognize him. And even if she heard his name, they'd call him

Paul Mackenzie here, not P.J.
Sherwood.

Hence, Penelope was free to go.
And she should. Her brother dearly
wished it. And yet, when Blair stepped
in closer to her, her breath stilled,
and she was fully aware of why her
departure had become problematic.

But, one dance with this man
wouldn't jeopardize their safety.
She'd be just as safe to-morrow as she
was to-day. That is, as long as she
didn't misstep.

And yet, even though her secret
might remain safe—her heart was an
entirely different story.

She swallowed hard, nearly
breathless, as he leaned down closer.
His eyes rested on her lips as he
pushed a rebellious strand of hair
behind her ear. Her heart raced.

"Uncle Blair," Elsie's voice splashed through the sweltry air. He straightened and jumped away from Penelope as he spun to greet his niece. "We've finished tending the horses."

Where was her fan when she needed it? She really should keep that article in her hand seeing how often its presence was required lately. She patted her cheeks in an attempt to conceal the redness that had surely leapt upon them.

"Elsie, we were on our way to you." He planted his feet a shoulder width apart. "Thank you for keeping her entertained, Lachlan."

"My pleasure." The man trailed Elsie, his demeanor calm, as he had been yesterday before he had realized her identity. "Thank you for your visit," he directed his words at her. "I'm certain Fiona is most obliged, and I'm certainly glad to put this whole misunderstanding behind us. Blair's correct, coming here certainly required you to possess a wealth of courage."

A wealth of courage? She glanced at Blair. He had certainly spoken well of her. A bashful smile lit his lips. Hastily, she turned her sheepish grin on Lachlan. "I'm only too pleased you've both accepted my apology. And congratulations on your betrothal. Fiona spoke of your courtship and you seem perfectly matched. I do hope you shall both be famously happy."

"Thank you." He eyed Blair. "But now that I'm to be a married man, I must attain a bride for my cousin, so he can be as overjoyed as I am." He slapped him on the back.

"Uncle Blair, are you to be married?" Elsie dropped her freshly picked daisy. "I shall be most delighted if you wed Penny." Her bright, little eyes darted between them.

"Elsie," Lachlan's laughter ended the silence. "Your uncle Blair hasn't made his intentions known." Penelope froze. Did Blair have *intentions*? Toward her?

"But, can it not be, Penny?" Elsie's face scrunched in absolute confusion.

"It most certainly can." Lachlan nodded with a smirk. Penelope's cheeks flamed red hot.

"Wonderful." Elsie grinned. "Penny embroiders exceptionally well."

"Thank you," she managed an awkward squawk.

"I shall duly note that my future wife must be proficient at embroidery," Blair teased. "But should possessing that skill be of the utmost priority in my search for a wife?"

"Nay, there are plenty of skills and traits you must insist she possess," Elsie spoke with such an air of particular seriousness her sweetness etched a permanent smile on each adult. "We must compose a list at home."

"Brilliant idea." Blair draped his arm over her small shoulders.

"I'd wish nothing more than to see that list to-morrow," Lachlan told Elsie conspiratorially, before he winked at Blair.

"Certainly," she eagerly proclaimed. "And if we've forgotten something, you can revise the list."

"Elsie," Blair cut in. "I believe 'tis past time we leave Lachlan and Fiona to rest before their special day to-morrow."

"Shall you be attending the wedding, Penny?" Elsie took her hand.

She nodded. "Have you chosen your dress?"

"Nay." She hadn't thought that far ahead. "Perhaps you can help me?"

"Absolutely." Her eyes lit up. "And at home, I shall show you the dress Uncle Blair gave me to wear."

She fought to keep her glance away from him as she smiled down at the darling little lass. "I cannot wait to see your uncle's choice of clothing. I'm sure 'tis lovely, and I do indeed wish to see it."

Blair coughed, then bid Lachlan farewell. They in turn followed his lead, and soon they were on their way home.

Home?

Blair and Elsie's house wasn't her home. And yet, as he helped her down from the wagon his hands were warm and inviting, familiar and welcoming. But she ought not feel such a longing to make this her home. Nor allow herself to feel that pang in her chest whenever he was near.

She sighed. She couldn't deny the extent to which she cared for him. He took excellent care of his niece, he was a fair employer, and he treated his prisoners of war with kindness. Not to mention, he was smart, thoughtful, charming, and beyond handsome. To name only a few of his finest traits.

She sighed, knowing full well they could never advance past mere friendship. And even that connection was uncertain, considering the secret she was keeping from him. That deception tainted everything.

And yet, as they left Mickey to tend the horses, and entered the house, she dilly-dallied behind as he lead Elsie to his study. She couldn't stop herself from desperately yearning for their predicament to be altered. Elsie believed he needed a list to find his perfect wife, but she didn't require such a list, he was her ideal husband. And when he glanced back at her, her heart raced.

Her mind slammed to thoughts about the kiss she wished would have caressed her lips if Elsie and Lachlan hadn't interrupted them. She put a hand to the doorframe to secure her wobbly legs. "I shall go see to tea."

She left before they could protest. A moment to right her thoughts was more than needed, because all this dreaming about him was pointless. He would never be hers.

Blair watched as Penny sashayed from the room. He longed to go with her. If she was to leave to-morrow, their time together was dwindling away at an alarming rate. He took a deep breath. What was he to do?

"Uncle Blair." Elsie tugged on his sleeve and yanked his attention toward her. "You look at Penny the way Lachlan looks at Fiona."

His eyebrows shot up. "I do?"

She nodded. "And Lachlan and Fiona are to be wed because they love one another. Lachlan told me so."

"He did, did he?" A grin spread.

"Aye. He said, 'First a man and woman become fond of one another, that causes them to fall in love, and then they're married.'"

"That may be how their love came to pass, but don't suppose those are the exact steps that lead to every marriage."

Her lower lip pouted out. "Why?"

He chuckled, "There are too many reasons to list."

"List!" She patted the paper on his desk. "We have yet to begin our list. I promised to show Lachlan tomorrow."

"Then we must begin posthaste." He grabbed his quill pen in the most serious manner he could muster. "What shall I write?"

"Um—" she hesitated "—nice, the woman must be nice." He scribbled the letters down, along with every word that followed, "Smart, humorous, pleasant, playful—"

"And she ought to always express her gratitude with a proper thank you." He winked at Penny as she entered the room.

"Aye," Elsie agreed obliviously. "And, she ought to say please, as well." She leaned over the paper as he transcribed her dictation.

The tea things Penny held wobbled and clattered in the tray. He stole a look at her and his quill pen scraped the parchment creating a large splotchy mess. "Please add the word neat—" Elsie examined his mistake "—especially considering how you botched this list."

Laughing, Penny set down the tray. He blotted at the black blob. "Is that so?" He set his quill pen down.

Elsie nodded and backed away from him with an enormous smile. "Aye," she squealed and ran, as he jumped up to tickle her.

"Allow me to show you how messy I can truly be." He twirled her around to the sound of her laughter, as he disheveled her hair.

"Blair," Penny chastised him, stifling her amusement. "Do you not realize how much longer we shall need to brush Elsie's hair now?"

"I shan't mind—" Elsie giggled "—I enjoy you brushing my hair."

His heart caught in his throat. How would he ever broach the subject of Penny's upcoming departure?

"'Tis most sweet, thank you." She handed Elsie a biscuit before she poured their tea. "But I imagine you also enjoy your uncle or Halcyon performing the task?"

Penny's eyes held his as she handed him a steaming teacup. "Thank you," he said, but a smile didn't grace his lips. He might be grateful at her attempt to prepare Elsie for her departure, but he certainly wasn't happy about her leaving. If only she hadn't decided that parting was necessary. Her presence brought such happiness to their lives.

"Aye, I do delight in having Uncle Blair attempt to brush my hair."

"*Attempt?*" He reached to tickle her, but she fell to the side and avoided his fingers.

"Incorrigible," Penny laughed. "I for one shall enjoy my tea, and perhaps a biscuit, and I would advise you to consider joining me, Elsie—" she settled into a chair with her cup "—because after this, I regret to inform you, but you must be put to bed, so you'll be well rested for the wedding to-morrow."

He nodded. To-night, he wouldn't tell Elsie of Penny's looming departure. He would save that unpleasantness for to-morrow.

Although, he would pray her retreat home would never come to pass.

*   *   *

"Goodnight, Elsie." Penelope whispered, as she leaned down and kissed her forehead. "Sweet dreams, sweet lass." Her eyes welled as she stood, and she lingered longer than usual to gaze upon the slumbering child. This was her last night. The last occasion she'd have to tuck Elsie into bed. *God, why was Blair designated as P.J.'s warden?*

The answer appeared the moment she had issued the question—P.J. was safe here. And as much as that pained her, she was grateful. Blair was a remarkable man. And the mere thought of him produced a smile. With one last loving touch, she straightened Elsie's blanket, then forced her feet to amble to the door.

If only she could be honest with Blair. Perhaps he'd offer forgiveness, just as his father had with his mother. Hope rose in her chest.

But she couldn't simply reveal her secret, could she? She hazarded one final look at Elsie before she sauntered down the hall to her own bedroom. With a sigh she concluded the inevitable—she couldn't divulge the truth. Divulging such information could prove disastrous and she'd never gamble with her brother's life. Besides, Blair's position would be compromised. He'd be pressed to choose between his duty as a warden and her. And imposing such a dilemma on him would be completely unfair.

But she must do something. 'Twas unfathomable to leave here—to leave him—and attempt to forget his existence. She would never accomplish such a feat, especially given the fact that she didn't wish to ever forget him. She must right her wrong. He had become most dear to her. She strode past her bedchamber and slunk down the stairs.

Outside his study she hesitated to verify she could slip in unnoticed. *Thank You, God*. With a deep breath of relief, she closed the door quietly behind her, then marched to his desk.

Quickly, she found parchment and his quill pen, then wrote a letter that exposed the truth—her entire story. Her words came faster than she could write, but she pressed on until she had explained every last detail. Then she begged for his forgiveness. She needed to regain his trust, because otherwise, the consequence of not being able to hope for a future together made breathing difficult.

Satisfied with her effort, she kissed the parchment, then swiftly folded the letter and stowed away the writing instruments. She mustn't dawdle. She couldn't be caught. If he were to set eyes on the letter prematurely, her brother's life, and her own, not to mention his, would be thrust into jeopardy.

She rubbed her neck, shivering at the possible consequences, and her inability to determine how Blair might react to the truth. But 'twas time to execute the next phase of her plan. She poked her head out of the study. The coast was clear. She hurried to the kitchen.

"Evening, Halcyon." She entered the tidiest kitchen, ready for the morrow. "Are you not off to bed?"

"I am now. I've just finished me nightly routine." The cook clanked a dish atop a stack of similar ones, then rid herself of her apron and hung the garment on a peg. "I've been plagued by a headache from mid-day. I've fought it, but I fear 'tis finally sapped me."

"I wasn't aware of your discomfort." She stepped farther into the darkening room, lit only from the dying fire and a couple of candles that cast shadows on the stone walls. "You must retire posthaste. And rest assured, if anyone might require anything, I shall assume your duties. Can I be of any further assistance?"

"Nay, thank ye. I shall sleep soundly now." She managed a smile. "Although, I must tell ye, I shall indeed miss ye when yer gone."

"I shall miss being here, as well." She hugged her. Then pulled away as she grimaced, "I do apologize, but may I ask one final favor?" Halcyon arched a brow. "I assure you 'tis nothing arduous. I simply hoped you might oblige me by giving this letter to Blair to-morrow, once he returns home from the wedding reception?" She held forth the letter, praying for her acceptance.

If she were far enough away when he received her letter, then surely he'd realize her intention had never been to aid her brother in an escape. Then, once she was safely home in Newark, she would pen another letter, which she prayed would be met with forgiveness. Perhaps then, they could establish a new friendship. One not rooted in secrets. One that could develop into something more. Dare she dream of a courtship?

"'Tis hardly a favor," Halcyon chuckled. "Consider yer request done."

"Thank you." She hugged her once more. "I shall leave the letter in this cupboard, behind the teacups." She dropped the parchment into place. "Now, I've caused you to linger far too long. To bed with you." She shooed Halcyon away. "I pray your health is restored by morning."

"As do I," the cook smiled, then lumbered from the room.

Penelope stood alone, the stillness of the night matched the sadness that befell her. Wrapping her arms around herself, her eyes fell to the kitchen floor as she watched her feet shuffle over the cobblestones to a window where she peered out into the darkness. Her reason for departing was justified, she had to remind herself. 'Twas of the utmost importance to ensure P.J. remained unharmed.

And although Blair was a good man, perhaps withholding the truth from him for such an extended length of time would infuriate him. He had mentioned his father's anger and how his family had nearly been torn apart. Suppose he reacted with the same hostility?

"Penny, I fully expected that by this hour you'd have withdrawn to your room."

She spun on her heal. "Blair," she squealed. Her hand flew to cover her mouth. "You startled me."

"I apologize," he smirked. "'Tis never been my intention, and yet, I seem to habitually startle you."

She flashed him a smile. "You need not apologize."

He glanced about the room. "Is there any tea?"

"Nay, but allow me to fix you a cup." She darted forward.

"Nay." He strode to the hearth and poured the last of the heated water that sat on the mantle into a teapot. "Pray tell me, why are you not asleep?"

"I might ask you the same question."

"May I offer you a cup of tea?" He returned the kettle to the crane over the glowing, red-hot embers.

"Aye, please." She handed him the tea leaves. "However, you failed to answer my question."

"True." He took the leaves to the table along with the teapot and set about formulating their brew. "But you still have yet to divulge your reason for being here." A sly smile crept up his lips. She froze. Had he overheard her conversation with Halcyon? Was he aware of her letter sitting in the cupboard?

He stepped forward and she moved to block him.

Stunned laughter escaped his lips, "We shall need teacups. Unless you prefer to drink your tea in a way I'm not accustomed to?"

"I shall retrieve the cups." She turned away from his astounded expression and opened the cupboard just enough to reach her hand in and grab two vessels. "Please, sit. Enjoy a much needed rest." She accidentally slammed the cupboard shut.

His eyebrows clenched together. "If you insist." Hesitantly, he sat.

She paused to compose herself before she placed the China on the table. "Due to a headache, Halcyon's retired for the night. Ergo, I've designated myself responsible for the kitchen and any of her other duties."

"I see." He watched her pour their tea. "And is that your sole reason for not being abed?"

Her head shot toward him. His voice oozed of suspicion. "I came in preparation of my departure to-morrow." She strained to focus on her task. "To say goodbye, things of that nature." She shrugged in an attempt to be nonchalant. However, fearing failure she uttered, "But alas, 'tis your turn." She passed him a steaming teacup, then sat.

"My turn?" He stirred in sugar.

"Aye. To offer a response. Your cousin's wedding is to-morrow, and you have yet to retire for the night."

"Ah." His hand stilled as his troubled eyes rose to meet hers. "If I were to unburden myself, that may upset you."

Her voice vanished. She couldn't fathom him behaving in any way, or uttering anything, that would anger her. But then P.J. bounded to the forefront of her mind and she was sickened by thoughts of wardens and prisoners.

She forced down the lump in her throat, unable to remain silent a moment longer, "You may be correct—" she shifted in her seat "—however, you've now piqued my interest, so I must be told."

His eyebrow hitched and she bit the inside of her cheek. Where her brother was concerned, the wrong words habitually left her lips.

"Sorry, you needn't tell me," she changed her tune. "But I do wish you would." She squeezed her hands together under the table in wait of his reaction. "Perhaps unburdening yourself might offer you solace?"

"Perhaps," he mused. Then, most solemnly, he leaned forward. "If I confide in you, you must promise to never speak my words to another living being." His eyes grew dark. "You must take my burden to your grave."

She gulped.

"Those are my conditions—" his eyes burrowed into hers "—are you willing to enter into such a commitment?"

Eva Maria Hamilton

11

Blair stared hard into Penny's blue eyes. Her lips pinched together. His breathing ceased. Would she agree to his terms?

She nodded.

224

He jumped from his chair. The legs scraped across the wood floor. Reluctance ate his innards. Regret snaked around his gut. Whatever had possessed him to tell her his secret?

He paced the room. His fingers raked rigidly through his hair. He had already confided in her about his mother's past and her web of deceit. If he now confided this, surely she'd suppose his entire family riddled with madness—including him.

However, his urge to divulge his secret had a purpose. If she knew his secret, perhaps she'd stay. He stormed back to the table and plunked himself down. She had declared her wish to leave after the wedding reception tomorrow, hence the sands in their hourglass had neared their finale. Time had forsaken him. And try as he may, he was at a loss to produce additional reasons to entice her to remain.

"Penny, there are only three people who know what I'm about to tell you. And Halcyon and Mickey only know out of dire necessity, because I need their help." Her eyes didn't stray from his. "Pastor West however, has been my confidant through all of this. A better man, I know not." She reached out a hand and covered his.

He peered down at her delicate fingers. They did indeed belong entwined with his. "Penny." He turned her hand over and squeezed it. "I trust you." His eyes found hers again. "I know you shall never retell what I profess to you."

"I'd never," she promised.

He smiled. "Alas, now 'tis my turn to state that *I'm at a loss regarding where to begin*." She squeezed his hand back, but didn't utter a sound. She simply sat, poised to listen. Her encouragement warmed him. "I wish to make you acquainted with what lies beyond the barn." He took a deep swill of air.

She didn't flinch. In fact, she perked up. "I'm already aware that P.J. and Clyde's cabin is there." She released his hand and withdrew back into her seat.

"There's another log cabin." There, he had said it. "'Tis farther than P.J. and Clyde's."

"I believe I've seen the one you're speaking of," her voice fell as she looked at him under her lashes.

"You have?" 'Twas unfathomable for her to have obtained the knowledge of what lay in that cabin.

"Aye." She leaned in closer. "The night of the thunderstorm, when I assisted Halcyon in delivering *three* meals past the barn—" his mind blasted back to that night. She had fallen and he had carried her home. In his arms, she had cradled herself against him. She belonged there. With him. The world had made sense. His life. His future. Everything had felt right. His fingers clenched with the desire to hold her once more. "—I took two meals to the prisoners and Halcyon took the third meal farther."

"I see," he muttered, shaking away his previous thoughts.

"There's more." She winced, and a look of guilt settled on her face. "I believe I unearthed your secret much earlier than that night. Do you recall the first time I visited? I was invited for tea and you encountered me in the woods?"

He nodded.

She took a deep breath, then continued, "I had been running, because I had been frightened after I had stumbled upon a female prisoner that you have locked in that other cabin."

Wind escaped his lungs. Tension knotted his shoulders. He mustn't allow her to believe this falsehood any longer. "The woman I keep in that cabin is my secret. She's not a prisoner of war."

"She's not?" she gasped. "Then who, pray tell, is she?"

He rubbed the back of his neck. "'Tis a long story. Do you wish for another cup of tea?"

"Nay." She waved her hand in protest. "I most ardently wish for you to continue your explanation." He hesitated. "Please."

Slowly, he nodded. "As you wish." He folded his hands and asked God, not only for the strength to tell her, but for His help in assuring that she shan't be appalled, especially of him. "When Elsie was sent to me, I was informed she had been in a horrible nautical accident. Apparently, her parents had ventured out onto the water even after some nearby fishermen had warned them of a terrible storm that was fast approaching." She grimaced. "I fear the story only worsens." He fought the knots in his stomach. "Elsie's father was well aware of the storm. In fact, 'tis said he planned their boat trip to occur during the worst of it."

"What?" Her face contorted from confusion into one of pure disgust. "Why?"

"After Elsie had been living here a couple of months, more of the story was revealed. Not from Elsie of course, she refuses to speak of that day." Her eyes beseeched him to continue. "I still have yet to learn all the details of what happened on that despicable day, but I have pieced together much of what happened."

Her eyebrows creased with curiosity, but she said, "Do take your time. 'Tis obvious how painful this is for you to speak of."

"Thank you." He boldly took her hand. "Speaking of this with you—"

his eyes locked with hers "—is scary, but sharing myself with you feels natural."

Her hand weakened and her eyes swam with emotion. After a long moment, she uttered, "I'm glad." Then, abruptly, she straightened.

However, her hand remained in his, and that afforded him the courage to continue, "Where they had lived, a woman emerged very distraught by the death of Elsie's father, and more than one person confided that 'twas more than mere gossip and hearsay that she was Elsie's father's mistress."

"Nay?" Her shoulders dropped.

"I believe in this case the rumors were true. But we have yet to come to the worst part." He smoothed his fingers over the back of her hand. "According to people who knew this woman well, they told me she had been happily expecting Elsie's father to wed her."

"But, that's not possible," she roared. "He was already married, and they'd had a child."

"Precisely." He watched as understanding clouded her eyes. "'Twas widely whispered around that town that Elsie's father had attempted to kill his wife and child to free himself to marry once more." She recoiled away from him. "Only his plan failed, and he wound up dead."

"Along with Elsie's mother," she spat.

"Nay." He shook his head. "Elsie's mother is alive. My half-sister, Cindy, is the woman I house here in that other cabin."

Her jaw dropped.

"Cindy's body was found in the next village. She must have somehow managed to travel safely to shore, just as Elsie had."

"Thank, God."

"Aye, God truly worked through those people. They didn't know her from Adam, and yet, they nursed her back to health. Eventually they discovered from where she hailed, and all roads led back to me. But that took some time. Hence why she arrived here much later then Elsie."

She crossed her arms. "Pray tell, why did you allow me to assume that Elsie's mother was dead?"

"For the same reason I never told Elsie her mother had been found."

"Which is?"

An earnest need to plead his defense ignited his assertive tone, "Cindy's not the same woman she once was. She seemed so close to death when she arrived here. I believe now she has improved somewhat, but she still refuses to speak. Her hours are consumed by sitting listlessly. And she only reluctantly obeys commands from Halcyon when she's fed, bathed, or dressed."

"But, Blair—" her voice remained calm, but adamant "—she's alive."

"Aye, but please bear in mind what Elsie's state was when she first arrived. She was already in such deep anguish. I couldn't allow her to witness her mother in such a wretched condition after the wee lass had finally begun to calm herself and adjust to life here. And I didn't know if Cindy would even survive. I couldn't allow Elsie to lose her mother all over again if Cindy worsened and died."

He shivered, remembering how far Elsie had progressed from her first day here. He could only pray his sister would one day, as well. "I've sent for numerous doctors to examine Cindy, and none have succeeded in getting her to respond or show even a hint of emotion. Their best hypothesis is that she's in a severe state of melancholy causing petrification. 'Tis as if she's merely alive in a shell. And yet, in reaction to her husband's actions, how can more be expected?"

"Oh, Blair. This is far too great a burden for any one person to bear." She closed her eyes as she rubbed her forehead.

"Then please," he whispered. "Agree to stay."

Her eyes flew open and her gaze hit him, but her silence pierced him.

When she finally spoke, her features softened, "I shall pray for guidance." Her fingers reached forward and stroked his arm. Her touch soared his temperature. "And I shall pray for you, and for Elsie and Cindy, as well. But I cannot lie, I'm not in agreement with you keeping Elsie from her mother. However, I do understand your reasoning, and I shan't argue. God shall help, because *with God all things are possible*."

He dipped his chin. He appreciated her truthfulness, but her disagreement with his decision stabbed at his chest. She disapproved of his actions. Had his conduct been wrong? He didn't think so at the time, but now, perhaps he had errored.

"Blair, how much longer shall you carry this load?"

"I'm not sure. With my farm, the prisoners, Elsie and Cindy—"

Penelope's heart broke for him. "It certainly is more than enough to contend with. How do you even find time to think? Can you not foresee a way to alter your situation?"

"That's what I've been striving for. Having you here as Elsie's nanny has made a world of difference." He patted her hand, causing her palm to lie still on his bicep. "But now you are to leave. Please do reconsider. Although, come Monday, other facets of my load shall be lightened some."

"Good." She slipped her fingers free, unable to think properly whilst she touched him. "Are you able to hire more hands to help on the farm?" She gripped her teacup, but the China had cooled, and 'twas definitely a poor substitute for his warm skin.

"Nay, I shan't hire anyone new. But my responsibilities shall lessen, because my prisoners are to be sent south."

Her teacup slid out of her grasp and rattled in the saucer. "They're being sent away—from here?" she sputtered. "Away—from you?"

"Aye." His eyebrows pulled together.

"How awful. I cannot imagine them not being here. And I am in complete dread as to what may await them in the south." She shifted nervously in her seat. She ought not to have reacted with such vigor. But what would become of P.J? *God, why did You allow this to happen?*

"My responsibilities shall lessen without prisoners, which shall afford me more time here, with Elsie," he explained in apparent bewilderment. As he ought to, given her odd reaction. At first, she had advised him to lessen his load, and then she had contradicted herself. He must think her utterly ridiculous.

"Indeed, that shall lessen one heavy burden." She squeezed her hands under the table, but the shaking didn't cease. "I suppose I never considered you'd take such an action, considering what an exemplary warden you are. Suppose your prisoners are treated terribly farther south, what then?" She shook her head. "Not that their fate ought to be your highest concern." She bit her cheek. Nothing she'd said had come out properly. But then, she was more than flustered. She was terrified for P.J. "Forgive me, you ought to put Elsie first. She's a child and must be your first priority." She shut her rambling lips. Perhaps she'd do better to remain quiet and simply allow him to speak.

"I agree. And I do care for P.J. and Clyde. But I have my orders, and with all my problems, I don't see the need to contest them."

She nodded. She did understand his predicament. Nevertheless, she'd pray for God to somehow alter her brother's circumstances.

"But, rest assured, I shan't forsake them. I shall continuously send inquiries to learn of their situation."

"That is good of you. But, that hardly equates to the same level of care." She wished to slap her hand over her mouth. Her ability to suppress her repugnance of this new scheme was severely lacking. Her brother would be aghast at how badly she was handling their secret.

"Nay, I suppose you are correct. However, I must modify my schedule to allow more time with Elsie and Cindy."

"Aye, of course. I apologize for uttering such silly comments. Perhaps I'm overtired." She covered a yawn with the back of her hand. "I hope you shall excuse me, but I believe 'tis past time I retire for the night." Abruptly, she rose before he could answer. "I'm glad Elsie shall be blessed by more of your presence. And I shall pray your sister recovers."

"Thank you." His features contorted into confusion as she fled the room.

*   *   *

Penelope hadn't enjoyed a moment of sleep. Last night's conversation with Blair had whirled her thoughts into a tornado.

To assure her brother would remain safe, she had been completely adamant about leaving. However, if he wasn't here, perhaps she could remain? Her urge to stay in the United States had grown amazingly strong last night. She now, more than ever, desperately wished to help Blair mend his family. And yet, not knowing how P.J. would be treated farther south, she had half a mind to follow him. She most certainly was at a crossroad.

Hence, she urgently needed to speak with her brother. And as soon as dawn broke she slipped out of the house and ran to the prisoners' cabin. "P.J.," she whispered, praying Clyde still slept so she could converse with her brother privately. "P.J.," she repeated a tad louder into the opening where she had passed his food.

"Penny?" his voice croaked. "What's the matter?" Her response lodged in her throat. "Why have you come? Are you in danger?"

"Not imminently." She huddled close to the wall.

"Then return home before anything terrible happens," he urged in a hushed tone.

"But you may be in danger."

"What?" concern edged his voice. She stared at the wall as if she could peer directly through their dwelling and see him. "Penny, pray tell me everything."

"Of course," she stammered. "Blair confided in me that on Monday morn, you and Clyde are to be sent farther south—"

"South," Clyde roared. She bit her lip.

"Penny," P.J.'s voice rushed forth. "You mustn't ever consider traveling south alone. Please, heed me. 'Tis much too dangerous. Go home."

She held onto the wall for support. "You cannot expect me to

simply return home and leave you. What
if they torture you?"

"I shan't see you hurt," he
hissed. "Promise me you shan't travel
south, especially alone." His words
hung in the air between them.

"Fine," she mumbled. If her
brother was to be confronted with more
than his share of trouble, she ought
not add to his suffering by causing
him to fret about her.

"Good. Now, return home."

Home? She rested her forehead
against the log cabin. "If I remain
here, Blair has assured me he shall
inquire after you. I cannot forfeit
being privy to such information."

"Could you not write to him from
Newark? From there, you'd be safe.
Perhaps you might even reveal the
truth to him, without the risk of your
being hurt?"

In a whimper of defeat, she
sighed. Leave Blair? And Elsie?
Unconscionable.

"Penny, I know you better than
anyone. Is there another reason you
wish to remain here?"

She quivered. Had he deduced her feelings for Blair? "Blair and Elsie are still very much in need of my services."

"I see," his voice came devoid of harshness. "But suppose you remain, and Blair discovers you're my—" he barred the word *sister* from escaping his lips. And duly so, since Clyde was notably afoot with his tirade of rants continuously rumbling to the fore.

"I understand, but my mind is a muddled mess, making me absolutely indecisive." She squeezed her eyes shut.

"Have you considered that Blair may never offer you his forgiveness?"

She gulped. Aye, she knew her feelings could be thwarted and never returned. Not only had she hidden this secret, but the sheer length of the concealment would aggrieve him.

"Penny, you must promise me that if you remain here you shan't tell him about us. I don't presume to know how he might react, but if 'tis abysmal, I shan't wish you under his rule. You must allow me to leave here without that heaviness on my mind."

She pushed away from the wall. At last, her determination was resolved. "I shan't divulge a word."

A harsh grunt escaped his lips. "Then, you've resolved to stay?"

"I must."

"If you believe it best," he resigned. "But I still firmly believe you ought to return home."

"I'm sorry. I cannot. Please understand." She swallowed the words *I love you*, since she had already spoken with an excess of candor before Clyde. "Take care of yourself, P.J."

"You take care of yourself." She winced at his words. "Goodbye, Penny."

"Goodbye," she sobbed, stepping away from the wall. The farewell burned in her throat, as she ran back to Blair's house and straight to her bedchamber.

*   *   *

After Blair finished his chores, he rushed home to dress in his finest clothes. The day couldn't have been more pleasant for Fiona and Lachlan's wedding. 'Twas warm, but not overly humid, and large, puffy, white clouds sailed happily through the sky.

All of nature seemed alive with cheerfulness, and he prayed he could join them. But that rested solely on Penny's decision to stay. And he wouldn't be privy to that until he spoke with her. *God, please answer my prayers and provide her with whatever inducement she requires to stay.*

He shrugged into his blue tailcoat and headed downstairs. "Good morning," he greeted her and Elsie. "I dare say I have the honor of being in the presence of two of the most beautiful ladies in the world." As he strolled down the corridor toward them, he was struck by the alluring manner in which Penny's blue empire waist gown illuminated her eyes. And his heart thumped hard in his chest at the thought of requesting a dance with her at the wedding reception.

She dipped a curtsey. "Good morning."

Elsie ran to him. "Uncle Blair," she took his hand. "Do you not think Penny is particularly beautiful?" She dragged him closer to her nanny.

"Nay," he answered, unable to take his eyes from Penny.

"Pardon?" Elsie looked over Penny's appearance, then settled an angry glare upon him. "Why ever not?"

"Because—" he cracked a smile "—every time I have the pleasure to behold her, she is beyond beautiful, not merely today."

"Oh," a spark lit in Elsie's eyes and her word was thus exaggerated. Then she turned to Penny, "Do you not think my uncle is exceedingly handsome?" His niece took her hand.

"Most dashing." A redness rose to Penny's cheeks.

"Good," Elsie grinned. Then quickly joined Penny's hand to his before she ran from the house.

His fingers melted into Penny's, as the warmest blue sea shined up to meet his eyes. "My niece is well-nigh on her way to becoming a bona fide matchmaker."

She blushed as she pulled her fingers away. Akin to a child who had tasted sugar for the first time, he wished for more, yearned for her soft touch, to have her fingers entwined with his—

"I believe you may be correct," she chuckled.

"And if she is a true proficient, I shan't wish to discourage her."

Her cheeks deepened in color. "I suppose we ought to set forth. I shan't wish us to be late."

"Indeed." He held out his arm. A smile spread across his lips as her hand slipped perfectly into place. "Penny." He stopped just after they had exited the house. "I know we must hurry to the church, but I did hope we might eke out some time alone to talk?"

She lifted her chin until her eyes met his. "Regarding our conversation last night?"

"Regarding your decision to return home."

"My, don't ye make an attractive pair." Halcyon came around the corner of the house carrying a bucket of water. "Ye'd better take heed though, Blair. Every lucid, unmarried gentleman shall attempt to fill Penny's dance card," she gave him a knowing look as she strode past them into the house.

Heat clawed up his neck. Aye, if the men had eyes, competition ought to be fierce. But he stood primed to battle for her attention.

"Is she not attending the wedding?" Penny peered over her shoulder at his cook's retreating form.

"Nay," he whispered. "She and Mickey are to remain here for Cindy's sake."

"Oh, aye, indeed." She turned back to him with a mixture of pity and agony on her face. "And to mind the prisoners, as well."

He shook his head. "Actually, Clyde and Paul are to join us. But unfortunately, the clothes I ordered have yet to arrive and they must wear their British uniforms. I do regret that, but I shall send their clothes on to them in the south. Perhaps they shall still be of use there."

"You're bringing your prisoners to the wedding?"

"Just for the ceremony. I shan't wish to leave them locked up for an entire day and night."

"They must certainly appreciate the inclusion." She looked out toward the forest where the cabins lay. "I suppose 'tis yet another reason I believe it sad they shan't stay with you. You're a most benevolent warden."

"Thank you for your kind words, but—"

"I apologize, my intention wasn't to saddle you with feelings of guilt. I understand why you must send them south. I simply wish a better option would present itself." He nodded, and she muttered, "If only this war had never begun."

He patted her hand. "The longer the fighting persists, the more people I believe agree with that sentiment."

"I pray those with the power to end this war, do so, before more lives are destroyed."

"Aye." He prayed for that every night.

"You must excuse me. Here I am rambling on when we ought to be hurrying to the church. Shall we?"

"Aye." He led them to the wagon. "Elsie, please sit in front between Penny and I and leave the back for the prisoners." he called her away from the horses and lifted her into the wagon before he took Penny's hand and helped her into her seat.

The smoothness of her skin gave him pause. How he wished spending time together during this excursion meant as much to her as it did him, because he wished for nothing more than to become more attached to her.

Penelope's stomach churned each time the wagon hit a dip in the road. 'Twas incomprehensible that this day and the next were the only ones that remained until her brother was lost to the south. She couldn't speak with him now in the wagon and with the multitude of wedding guests sure to be milling about, 'twould be nigh impossible to eke out a moment alone with him. Not that she wasn't determined to try.

Just as, she shan't lose hope or cease her efforts in discerning a feasible way to keep him here. She mustn't appear overly obvious though in wishing P.J. to remain, or Blair's interest would be piqued, and then his suspicion would reign. For all intents and purposes, she ought not care to such a large extent what became of his prisoners.

She glanced at Blair. His polished black boots matched his top hat and his grey drop front trousers fit him as if they had been tailored especially for him. Under his blue coat, his white cravat was tied with grand proficiency.

He was, without a doubt, the most handsome man she had ever laid eyes upon. And yet, appearances aside, he possessed an overabundance of admirability. She had known her heart belonged to him the moment she had learned he had taken sole responsibility for the care of his niece.

"We've arrived," he interrupted her thoughts. Turning his head, a grin spread across his lips as he caught her observing him. She darted her eyes away, her cheeks ablaze. "And I do believe we're in the nick of time," a humorous lilt accented his words, as he pulled the horses to a stop at the end of a long line of wagons and carriages.

"I'm filled with enough happiness to burst," Elsie squealed, clapping her hands.

Her elation brought a smile to Penelope's face. "Elsie, suppose we seat ourselves whilst your uncle manages the horses and his prisoners?"

"May we?" She bounced in her seat.

He nodded, exchanging an amused look with Penelope before he jumped down to help them from the wagon.

"Please don't tarry though, Uncle Blair," she proclaimed in earnest. "I shan't wish you to miss a thing. You must learn the lot before you marry."

He laughed, as he leaned down to kiss her sweet head. "I shan't miss this for all the world." He stood to his full height and turned his sights on Penelope. She felt the heat from his gaze. "I hope the wedding pleases you," his voice grew deeper as he stepped closer to her. "Perhaps the ceremony shall inspire you." He winked and her heart fluttered. *Inspire her?* "And to be absolutely clear, so as to destroy any confusion that may remain regarding my earlier comment, you are strikingly beautiful."

Strikingly beautiful? She was most definitely struck. Before his amorous eyes, she was utterly astonished. However, in a whisper, she somehow sputtered, "Thank you." His grin widened.

"I see the bridegroom," Elsie shrieked.

She tore her eyes from him, but her heart continued to race and she required more than merely her fan. Later, she had promised to speak with him, but considering she could hardly breathe at the thought of being alone with him, how would she force any words out?

She reached for Elsie's hand, not daring to even peek at him again. "Shall we greet the other guests before the ceremony begins?"

"Aye, please." Elsie skipped beside her as they set off.

Penelope habitually found herself searching for Blair and P.J. in the crowd, as Elsie's cheeks were pinched by relatives, and she received hugs with such strength the little lass must have suffered from a lack of air.

"She's adorable in that yellow gown," Blair's voice came from behind.

A warm tingle shoot through her. "Aye, she's darling," she stammered, unable to speak correctly as he drew even closer. "Pray tell, where are your prisoners?" She peered past him into the field. With such a vast amount of people to greet, they had neared the church, but as of yet, they still hadn't managed to step foot in the door.

"Seated with my uncle Duncan." She felt his eyes upon her, even though she didn't trust herself to return his gaze. "I've spoken with the bridegroom, and Lachlan told me his bride has been delayed."

"Is all well?" she asked in alarm.

"Aye." He grinned. "I only hoped the information might persuade you into beginning our conversation."

She swallowed. "Certainly," her nerves rattled her voice and betrayed the calm exterior she had tried to hide behind.

"Shall we take a turn about the lawn?"

She nodded, then hugged herself as she fell into step beside him.

"Earlier, Halcyon brought a matter to my attention that I wish to discuss," he began.

Air escaped her. Her muscles tightened as if she had plunged into the frigid waters of the Niagara River during winter. She had plumb forgot about the letter she had instructed the cook to give him after the wedding. Had Halcyon mistakenly surrendered her correspondence to him prematurely?

12

"Pray tell, what matter did Halcyon bring to your attention?" Penelope choked her words out, as all the ramifications of Blair knowing her secret crashed through her mind.

"She was entirely correct, you truly are lovely, and your dance card is sure to be immediately full. Hence, I shan't wish to be presumptuous, but I must ask, please do me the honor of being your partner for the first and last dance."

Air rushed back into her lungs. And determination coursed through her veins. Since she had chosen to stay, she must return home before him and destroy that letter. He must never lay eyes on it.

"I'd be honored to save those dances for you." Her heart warmed thinking of how he had appeared nervous to broach the subject.

He bowed, then took her hand and kissed it. His eyes gazed into hers. A wave of adoration swept her away. But she mustn't allow her brain to cease functioning. She fought the tide. She couldn't return his affection, if that was his intention, she feebly reasoned. She must win this battle and not allow any reciprocal telltale signs to be displayed, even though they threatened to burst forth with a vengeance. She couldn't begin their courtship whilst she kept a secret from him. Especially not a secret of this magnitude.

Taking a deep breath, she smiled and slipped her hand free, before she spun on her heel. Such odious complications.

"Have I somehow offended you?"

"Nay." She turned back, abhorred by the hurt and confusion painted on his face. "I'm sorry." She placed a hand on his arm and searched his eyes. Did he harbor feelings for her deep enough to withstand the truth?

She truly hoped so. But she mustn't probe. Now was not the time. She had promised her brother she shan't reveal her secret until she was firmly back on British soil.

However, when he took her hand and squeezed it, she sucked in a sharp breath. Possessing the knowledge they ought to remain purely as friends, and ensuring her heart responded in accordance, equated to the likelihood of her attempting to school a mountain lion to befriend a chicken.

"I do wish you to stay." He stepped in closer and took hold of her arms. "Please consider altering your plans?" She stared into his eyes and saw only tenderness. "I would cherish the opportunity to become better acquainted."

She bit the side of her cheek. If he attempted to kiss her, perhaps she ought to blockade her mind and listen to her heart? One kiss shan't hurt.

Aye, it would, she chastised herself. Having to live with only the memory of that kiss would surely grow to become a recipe for torture. And besides, 'twould be most unfair to him. He was completely unaware of her true identity.

"I sincerely wish for that, as well," she sputtered.

He drew her in even closer. Her breath escaped her. She sank into his embrace. Contentment washed over her. Any attempt at a rebuttal was futile. She loved Blair McAllister and she did indeed wish to kiss him—to melt into him and become one. And gazing up into his adoring eyes, 'twas evident his feelings were identical. How utterly perfect.

He held her tighter as his lips descending toward hers. "Thank you for allowing me this chance," his breath whispered into her lips.

But she hadn't been completely honest with him. "I'm sorry. I must go." She freed herself from his embrace. If she refused to be truthful with him, then she mustn't allow anything to transpire.

She trotted back to the church. Tears welled. If only she had met him under different circumstances.

Blair watched as Penny ran from him. His attempt to kiss her had most certainly not achieved the desired effect. He rubbed his finger under his cravat, feeling the heat of his frustration. What had possessed him to take such liberties? Had he not just confided how his mother had suffered whilst she worked for a man that desired her? His stomach tightened with repulsion. He was by no means similar to Cindy's father. But if Penny didn't harbor the same feelings for him, perhaps following this debauched encounter she'd be scared to be under his employ, and would most certainly return to Upper Canada. That tore at his heart.

He pushed his hat down harder on his head and trailed her back to the church. At the reception, his primary duty would be to mend this situation. He shan't allow this misunderstanding to ruin their connection. He ardently loved her and wouldn't be the agent who propelled her to return to Newark. The region was unsafe and he'd never forgive himself if calamity befell her.

Penelope met her brother's eye as she walked to her pew and settled into the seat next to Elsie. After the ceremony, she'd contrive some tactic to speak with him before Blair commanded he be returned home.

Blair. Her hand covered her flaming lips. How she wished things between them were different and she was free to love him. *God, please help me. S*he prayed until she had located him. Such a dear man. A smile tipped up her lips as she observed him assist a hobbling, elderly woman to her seat.

God couldn't have created a kinder or gentler man.

"The eleventh hour is upon us." Blair squeezed Lachlan's shoulders, as his cousin stood before the altar awaiting his bride. "Ready to proceed?"

"I've waited for this day my entire life."

"God bless you and your marriage." He hugged him, and over his shoulder, his eyes locked with Penny's—again.

She had been staring at him since he had entered the church. Hope rose in his chest. Perhaps she did love him and hadn't permitted him to kiss her for some other reason. He would continue to pray that somehow she would change her mind and stay.

*   *   *

"Is not Fiona a most beautiful bride?" Elsie sighed as they exited the church.

"She most certainly is." Penelope swung the little lass' hand.

"And her and Lachlan shall live happily together evermore."

"I pray they enjoy a lifetime of joy." She released Elsie's hand to open her parasol against the summer sun.

"With a whole brood of children," the lass giggled.

"If those children resemble you even one morsel—" she tweaked her nose "—they shall be blessed."

Remarkably, her grin widened. "Oh, Penny, may I tell Fiona how beautiful she is?"

"Certainly," she laughed as Elsie skipped away to deliver her message. She however didn't follow. Seeing that Blair stood next to Lachlan and Fiona, she refused to approach him. At least, not yet. Not until she could explain why she had run from him.

When his gaze met hers, she averted her eyes. *How foolish.* She mustn't simply stand there and ogle him. She had already stared at him excessively throughout the wedding. He was bound to think her one extremely confused woman after how she had left him before the ceremony.

Nevertheless, a smile crossed her lips as she relinquished the crowd and walked to a desolate side of the church. She'd most certainly cause him much happiness later, once she revealed her plan to stay.

However, as quickly as her smile had broadened, it vanished. Someone grabbed her arm and tugged her behind the church. She whimpered in pain. "Quiet," Clyde charged. "Or I shall truly cause you agony." She winced as his fingernails dug into her flesh.

"What is the meaning of this?" Frantically, she searched for help. However, with the wedding guests on the other side of the church they were isolated, unable to be seen or heard.

"Clyde, remove your hands from her at once." P.J. stormed toward them.

"I'm finished listening to you, Paul," Clyde spat venom. "I'm taking charge now." He shoved her toward P.J. and exposed a pistol.

"How did you acquire a gun?" Her brother shielded her.

"I suppose I'm smarter than I appear," he cackled. "Blair's uncle

Duncan shall realize that when he awakes to a rather large bump on his head. Now quiet. Henceforth, I shall be the one to speak."

He waved the pistol around. "The nicknames you two have for one another, coupled with the expanse of your concern for each other, signifies to me that you're more than mere acquaintances. The details however matter not to me. I only care how this shall benefit me." He hit his chest. "Which, by the way, thank you for the warning regarding our being sent south. And consequently, here's what I propose."

She shuddered, as Clyde switched the aim of his pistol from her chest to her brother's with each subsequent assertion, "You don't wish to witness his death, and likewise, he doesn't wish to watch you die. But don't fret. Neither of you shall die, *if* you act in accordance with my instructions."

"And what pray tell are those?" P.J. spoke through clenched teeth.

A wretched grin appeared on Clyde's face. "I'm glad you asked," he chuckled. "I'm not venturing south.

Hence, you shall both be aiding my escape back to Upper Canada." Her stomach twisted. The fault of this situation lay entirely with her.

P.J. shook his head. "That's exceedingly dangerous."

"Be that as it may, but this is the only option that has presented itself," he grew dead serious. "You must understand that if you refuse, that shall force me to kill you, since I obviously cannot allow you to reveal my plan of escape." He glared at her brother. "Now then, we've wasted more than enough time. We must begin step one."

"Which is?" she blurted.

A wicked grin licked his lips. "We must distract everyone long enough to make our escape."

"And how, pray tell, is that to be accomplished?" her brother barked.

"Simple," he spoke as if to a belligerent child. "I shall set fire to the church. That ought to distract people long enough for us to escape, but we must leave posthaste." He glanced about. "Paul, fetch us a wagon. Penelope, stay with me." P.J.

hesitated. "Go!" Clyde pointed his pistol straight at her. "Or she dies."

"Don't hurt her, Clyde," P.J. seethed.

"Just do as I say and we shall forget this ever happened when we're back in Upper Canada. You might think I'm a lunatic now, but you shall come to appreciate my methods once we're home."

She took a couple steps back. Nay, she would never understand burning down the house of God or risking the perils of an escape.

"Stop! Don't move any farther," Clyde commanded. She froze, staring into his pistol. That made everything clear. She would be forced to help Clyde escape. Which meant saying goodbye to the Mohawk Valley and everyone here.

This wasn't happening. She didn't want to leave. She couldn't abandon Blair or Elsie. If she left now she would lose all hope of a relationship with Blair, even as a friend. Helping Clyde escape would render her Blair's enemy, and anything that had blossomed between them would be dead. She'd never be able to help reunite Elsie with her mother.

Not a soul would ever believe Clyde had forced her and her brother to help him escape, and Blair would be compelled to concede this had been her plan all along. He would despise her.

Her mind spun as Clyde grabbed her arm and dragged her toward the church. "Don't even think about screaming for help, because I shan't hesitate to kill you or Paul," Clyde sneered, as he pulled her from one spot to the next, igniting the church in several places from the outside before throwing torches into the church.

"Are we not fortunate there's been a severe lack of rain this summer," Clyde laughed. "The church's wood is incredibly dry, it shall burn to the ground before the men can even grab a bucket of water."

Her lungs filled with the scent of smoke as P.J. came beside them with a wagon. "Get on," Clyde snapped as he grabbed her parasol and flung her article into the fire, before he pushed her up into the wagon. "Paul, did anyone see you?" he asked, jumping aboard.

"Nay." P.J. shook his head. "They all still stood huddled around the bride and bridegroom, and I took the farthest wagon."

"Good." Clyde grinned. "Now, go," he commanded.

She looked back over her shoulder as the horses began to move, flames had already reached the roof. Surely, someone would see them before they escaped. Blair had to realize Clyde and P.J. were missing. Help had to come. She and P.J. couldn't be at Clyde's mercy. Only God knew what this madman was capable of. And what he would do to them.

"Fire," someone yelled and commotion spread through the crowd.

"Elsie, stay here with Fiona." Blair handed her into Fiona's outstretched arms, before running to help put out the flames that whipped the church walls.

Where was Penny? He ran searching through the crowd. "Is anyone still in the church?" he asked Pastor West.

"Nay, I was the last one out and I closed the doors behind me."

He nodded, then continued his search, as more flames and smoke billowed into the sky. He had seen her outside, but then she had disappeared. Guilt gnawed at him. If only he hadn't tried to kiss her, then there shan't have been any awkwardness between them and she shan't have been avoiding him.

"Uncle Duncan." Confusion seared Blair, when he spotted his uncle lying on the ground behind the church. "What has befallen you?" He cradled his uncle's head, seeing blood seep out of a gash on his forehead.

"Blair?" his uncle's eyelids fluttered open. "What happened?"

"I hoped you could tell me." He helped his uncle sit up.

"My head is pounding." His uncle reached up to hold it, disgust shading his features when he saw blood on his fingers. "Now I remember." He leaned on him to stand. "Clyde ambushed me."

"Clyde?" He gritted his teeth.

"He took my pistol."

A torrent of emotion exploded inside him as his eyes darted around, but he couldn't see Clyde or Paul in all the commotion. "Shall you be fine?" he asked his uncle.

"Aye, Blair. Go find yer prisoners."

He dipped his chin, and seeing Lachlan's mother nearby, he called for her. She turned toward them and the moment she saw Duncan concern ignited her features. "Did ye fall?" She took hold of Duncan.

"I shall explain once Blair leaves." Duncan nudged him. "I shall be fine. Go."

"If you're sure." He looked between them.

"I am," Duncan responded. "Now go."

He clapped his uncle on the back, then ran through the crowd. He needed to find Clyde before he harmed someone else. "Have you seen Clyde, Paul, or Penny?" he asked person after person and every time they responded that they hadn't.

Was Penny actually with Clyde and Paul? He ran back to Fiona and Elsie. "My prisoners have escaped," he huffed. "And Penny is missing."

"Penny's missing," Elsie shrieked. He cringed, realizing too late that he ought not to have admitted that news before her.

"I shall find them." He gripped his niece's shoulder. "Fiona, can you ask someone to take Elsie home. Halcyon and Mickey are there, they shall watch her until I return." He hated to task her with a favour on her wedding day.

"Of course," she didn't hesitate and he couldn't have been more grateful.

"But I don't want you to go," Elsie cried, grabbing hold of his tailcoat.

"I shan't be gone long." He knelt down to reassure her, but with the church burning to ashes behind him and Penny nowhere to be seen, he doubted anything but his presence could keep Elsie calm. And even then, watching the terror on her face, he wasn't sure even he could sooth her.

"Nay." Elsie crossed her arms. "Don't leave."

"Elsie, I'm sorry, but I must." Pain ripped his chest. His niece had already experienced too much with the loss of her parents. He could see the fear in her eyes. She thought she'd now lose him. "I promise I shall return as quickly as I can."

"Nay," Elsie shouted again. His heart tore. He had to go after his prisoners and determine where Penny had gone, but the thought of hurting Elsie overwhelmed him.

"Come now, Elsie, your uncle must perform his duties as a warden," Fiona tried to reason with her. But Elsie only glared with defiance.

"Aye. You may enjoy some cake, and dancing, and then upon my return, we shall enjoy another tea party." He tucked a loose strand of brown hair behind Elsie's ear. "So please go home and arrange everything for our tea." He took a step back.

"Nay," Elsie yelled, but when she tried to step toward him Fiona squeezed her back into a hug.

"I'm already anticipating all the fun we shall enjoy," he said, as he continued to back away. "Please save me a piece of cake."

"Uncle Blair." Elsie reached out her arms and struggled against Fiona, but Fiona held her tight, and although her distress hurt him, he went in search of a horse.

"But I love Uncle Blair," Elsie wailed and then slumped into Fiona's arms sobbing.

Blair rode down the main street of town with a vengeance. He loathed that he had been forced to hurt his niece. He pushed his horse to gallop faster as he said the same prayer he always did when his life was in danger. *God, please keep me safe so I may return home to Elsie.*

A crash sounded behind him and he turned to see the church roof collapse. Not much time remained before the walls would crumble, as well.

He growled. If Clyde and Paul had set fire to the church then he was responsible for its desecration. He needed to apologize to the town, and make amends by rebuilding the church. *I'm sorry, God. I shall right this wrong.* He had never suspected Paul could have behaved in such a manner.

And 'twas unfathomable that Penny had contributed to such destruction. But then, where were they?

He squinted, looking for any sign of his prisoners or Penny.

He saw nothing.

Although at this speed, he would near Fort Niagara soon. Then he would recruit help in capturing them, because he was certain his prisoners were attempting to escape across the Niagara River to return home to British land.

*   *   *

"Clyde, you cannot push this horse any farther." P.J. dropped the animal's front hoof. "He's limping because he's lost his shoe."

"Only you, Paul, would choose a wagon with a lame horse," Clyde sneered. "Penelope, exit the wagon at once."

She grabbed P.J.'s hand and jumped down, making sure to remain close to him, since Clyde was still threatening them with his pistol every chance he got.

"Paul, help me move this wagon behind those trees for cover, because I'm sure by now, Blair's after us and moving faster than we've been." Clyde mercilessly made the hobbling horse limp over some rocks. "Now untie the other horse. I shall be riding him."

She shivered. If Clyde was going to ride, did he expect them to run alongside or was this the end for them?

"Penelope, come here." Clyde waved her over with his pistol. "Do you see that horse coming down the road?" She nodded. "I believe that's our good friend, Blair," he scoffed.

She hid a smile. Blair would save them.

Then her stomach flipped.

What if Clyde took him by surprise and killed him instead?

*C*lyde grabbed Penelope's arm and squeezed with such force she immediately latched her mouth closed to keep from yelping in pain. "Wave at Blair to stop. Inform him you were travelling back to Upper

Canada—alone—but one of your horses lost a shoe. Then say you somehow untied the other horse, but that horse bolted. Feign ignorance about the church fire and especially about Paul and I escaping. And whatever you do, hinder Blair, because Paul's accompanying me, and should I encounter any trouble with Blair, I shall kill Paul."

She stared at Clyde. The coldness in his heart poured out of him and she didn't doubt his words. "I shall do anything, Clyde. Please, just don't harm P.J."

"His death is on you, Penelope. I'm returning to Upper Canada with him dead or alive. Now go and work your feminine wiles." He pushed her out of the shadow of the trees and into the blazing sun.

Her eyes fought to adjust to the brightness as Blair's horse thundered closer. "Penny?" His voice rose over a cloud of dust. "Why are you here?" His horse clopped to a halt in front of her.

"I was in a wagon, heading home, but one of the horses lost a shoe,"

her words raced out. She hadn't
lied—and she wouldn't—but she prayed
to God for help, because she couldn't
be the cause of Blair or P.J. getting
killed.

"Where's your wagon?" He looked
about.

"In the shade." She didn't point
in case P.J. hadn't ridden far enough
away yet.

He raked his fingers through his
hair. "Are you alone?"

"Aye."

He eyed her, and she gripped her
fingers behind her back, certain he
thought she had lied and her worst
fear had come true—he suspected her
of trying to help Clyde and P.J.
escape.

"Why have you not untied your
good horse?" He questioned her as if
she were his adversary. "Can you not
ride bareback?"

"That horse has already been
untied and 'tis gone."

"I see." A look of anguish
crossed his face. "I'm sorry, but I
shall return for you as soon as I'm
able." He turned his horse.

"Wait." She waved her arms. "I cannot remain here alone. Please, take me with you."

He stared at her. "Penny, my prisoners have escaped and I must pursue them."

"Then I shall accompany you." She stepped closer to his horse.

"'Tis too dangerous."

"'Tis just as dangerous for me to remain here stranded by myself."

He grimaced, but didn't move. She bit her bottom lip. He must concede, because standing here alone would render her useless in keeping him or P.J. safe.

"Fine." He jumped down to assist her. "Perhaps 'twould be best for you to be with me."

She nodded, but was seared with the pain of thinking he suspected her of such terrible wrongdoing that he needed to maintain a watch over her. However, if that kept her brother and him out of harm, she accepted his plan wholeheartedly. "Thank you." She seated herself on his horse, all the while thinking of a way to keep him away from Clyde and P.J. so she could keep them all safe.

Blair slid onto his horse in front of Penny. Her wanting to ride with him didn't hold water. If she had fled town to avoid him after his attempt to kiss her, then why would she be this eager to be with him now? And if she was helping Clyde and Paul escape, why was she alone?

But his unanswered questions must wait. "Ready?" He glanced back at her.

"Almost." She made slow work of righting her skirt and positioning herself.

He scratched his head. Did she not know they must hurry? "How about now?"

She slowly placed her arms around him. "Aye."

He set off full tilt. He didn't want her on this dangerous mission with him, but she was correct—far too many maladies could befall her if he had left her there alone. And that thought made his stomach ill. Had she only chosen to accompany him because he was the lesser of two evils?

He shook his head. Whatever her reason, at least now this allotted him time to ask her some questions. "Penny, why did you leave without saying goodbye?"

"I'm sorry, I believed it best."

"Did what transpired between us before the ceremony influence your decision?" He swallowed hard when she squeezed her arms around him tighter, apparently he had inadvertently signaled his horse to gallop faster. "I'm sorry if I rendered you uncomfortable. That wasn't my intention."

"I know."

"Then why such a hasty departure? You don't even possess your belongings?"

"May we stop? I can explain."

"Nay. I'm sorry." He blew out a breath and tightened his grip on the reins. There would be time to discuss the matter once he had captured his prisoners. "We're nearing Fort Niagara." He darted his gaze about, keen to spot Clyde and Paul, because after their escape, he shan't underestimate what his prisoners were

capable of. And if they were hiding in
wait of him, they could shoot Penny
and him dead off this horse.

"Why do assume your prisoners
came this way?" she asked.

"Because I believe they're
attempting to escape back home and
this would prove the shortest route."
He slowed his horse, searching
everywhere for Clyde and Paul. *God,
please help me find them before
something terrible happens.*

His horse was almost beside the
stone walls of Fort Niagara and still
he hadn't caught sight of them. If
Clyde and Paul had come this far, the
only thing separating them from their
home was the Niagara River.

He squinted through the sunshine.
"That must be one of my prisoners."

Her head shot around his
shoulder. "Which one?" She pushed
against him for a better look.

"I cannot see from this distance.
I merely see a British officer's
uniform."

"I believe 'tis Paul." She
squinted. "But then where's Clyde?"

He shrugged. "We shall deduce that once we capture Paul. Hold on." He signaled to his horse to move quicker.

"If that's Paul, please don't harm him." Her words struck him silent. Of course he shan't hurt Paul, or Clyde, by choice. How ill was her opinion of him? "Blair, Clyde is the prisoner you must fear, not Paul."

He cocked an eyebrow. "How did you come to such a conclusion?" his question hung in the air, unanswered, as his prisoner shot his stolen pistol at the armed American guards. He pulled back on the reins, stopping his horse suddenly. A round of musket shots responded, clouding the sky before them.

Penny's arms slid away from him when the body of the man in the British officer's uniform slumped to the ground. "Nay," she screamed.

He tried to reach behind him and grab her, but she had already propelled herself off his horse. "Penny, stop." He jumped down and raced after her. "You cannot run in front of a group of armed guards."

She fought him. Tears streamed down her cheeks. "Unhand me, Blair. I must see to him."

He held her more firmly, guiding her back toward his horse. "He's gone, Penny. You cannot offer him any useful aid now." He wished to God, Clyde and Paul had never run off. This wasn't how he wished either of their lives to end. "We must go, Penny." One of his prisoners was still missing and he needed to find him before that prisoner met with the same fate.

"Nay. I shan't leave him." She struggled to free herself and he had never seen her this discomposed, not even after she had nearly been hit by that wagon. Her blue eyes were wild and he used everything he had to keep her with him.

"Blair, unhand me this instant," she wailed, as if he were smothering her to death. He shook his head and pinned her more securely against him. He wouldn't let her get herself killed. "You cannot keep me away from Paul." She fought harder. "He needs me. My brother needs me."

"Your brother?" He glared at her.

She froze. "Aye, Blair," she fumbled. "Paul's my brother." He went numb. She slumped to the ground and cried, "I've wanted to tell you countless times, but I couldn't. I promised P.J. He believed that divulging our connection was too dangerous. I couldn't put my brother's life in jeopardy, hoping selfishly that maybe you'd come to care enough about me to believe I never came here with the intention of helping him escape." She sobbed and wiped at her tears, "But now that P.J.'s dead, if you don't believe me, then I'm the only person you can hurt and I shall suffer the consequences. It matters not now?"

"On the contrary, but we shall discuss that later." He rubbed a hand over his face. "I'm sorry, but you must climb back on my horse. I must find my other prisoner before he's killed, as well." She didn't argue as he assisted her back onto his horse. Her behavior was reminiscent of his sister, and he cringed, fearing her brother's death would launch her into a life as a shadow of her former self.

He pushed away the awful thought, and once he sat astride, skimmed over the land. His prisoner must be close. "Penny, hold on," he yelled over his shoulder the moment he spotted the man. Thankfully, she tightened her grip. When they approached the horseman, he was surprised the man didn't bolt and actually dismounted.

"P.J.," she called, relief flooded her voice. "Did Clyde hurt you?"

With his hands raised, Paul shook his head, "Nay. Are you hurt?"

Tears streamed down her face anew and she hiccupped, "I'm fine. Better than fine, seeing you're alive—"

"Blair," Paul interrupted. "Please, allow us to explain."

"Aye, Blair." She nervously removed her hands from around his waist. He sat quietly to listen. "Clyde stole a pistol from someone at church and threatened to kill us if we didn't aid his escape. But the wagon Clyde made P.J. borrow didn't take us all the way to the Niagara River, because one of the horses lost its shoe, and that's when Clyde spotted you, and ordered me to keep you from catching them or he'd kill P.J."

"But your horse was faster than ours," Paul took over the explanation. "So Clyde chose to sacrifice me to you, so he could sneak back to Upper Canada—" His eyes grew distant at Clyde's horrendous end.

"Paul, are you armed?" Blair demanded.

"Nay." He held his arms up higher. "I never intended to escape and Penny didn't wish to help Clyde either. I'm glad and willing to return with you."

"Don't move." He kept his eyes on Paul, as he dropped off his horse. His prisoner obeyed whilst he cautiously searched him for weapons. None presented themselves. "Get back on your horse, Paul. I shall tie your horse to mine, then we shall return to the abandoned wagon and these two horses shall pull it. Hopefully, the lame horse can manage to walk slowly home if we wrap his hoof."

Sitting rigidly on their horses, the siblings exchanged terrified looks as he joined the horses together. "Did one of you set fire to the church?" he asked after he had finished.

"Nay, Clyde was responsible for that heinous act," Penny winced. "Were you able to save it?"

"Nay," he answered flatly, unable to grasp the entirety of the disaster that had ensued because he had allowed his prisoners to escape. If only he hadn't allowed Paul and Clyde to attend the wedding. Emotions tore through him like a tornado. But he steeled his mind. *Enough.* He must make haste. "Elsie was rather upset by today's events. I must return to her."

Tears glistened in Penny's eyes. "I'm sorry, Blair."

But he set off without another word. *God, please give me strength.*

*   *   *

"Blair, ye're home. Thank Ye, Lord," Halcyon shouted, as her and Mickey ran to meet the wagon. "Elsie's gone." His heart stopped. "I put her to bed, but later when I peeked in on her, she was missing."

He jumped off his horse. "Mickey, can you lock Paul in his cabin and deal with these horses." He tossed him the keys. "That one with the wrapped hoof has lost his shoe."

"Sure." Mickey took Paul away.

"Blair, I'm sorry. We've looked everywhere." Halcyon twisted her hands in her apron. "I cannot reckon where she's taken herself."

He grasped Halcyon's shoulders. "I shall find her." He needed to hear the certainty in his own words, because the sun was setting, and after darkness descended, if they hadn't found Elsie, the nocturnal animals that preyed on this land surely would."

"Blair, I shall accompany you," Penny's voice startled him. "Two sets of eyes are better than one."

"Fine." He hadn't had a moment to think, but one thing he knew he never had to question was Penny's love for Elsie. She couldn't have fabricated that. "Halcyon, please stay here incase Elsie returns." She nodded and he strode to the stable with Penny in tow.

"Where do you suppose she went?"
Penny asked.

"I wish I knew." He raked his
fingers through his hair. "With the
church being burnt down, my leaving,
and you going missing, she was
immensely distraught—" He stopped
when her hand took hold of his arm.

"I'm sorry, Blair. I didn't wish
to leave." She pulled her hand back
when he didn't respond. "But you're
correct, now isn't the time to discuss
this. We must find your niece." She
toed the dirt underfoot. "Poor Elsie,
she must feel abandoned again."

"Aye." His niece had suffered
immensely.

"Do you suppose she'd attempt to
find you?"

He shrugged.

"You don't suppose she'd venture
to Upper Canada to find me?" She
placed her hand over her chest, a look
of utter fear and dismay wrinkled her
face.

"I hope not." He quickly saddled
a horse for her before he led two
horses out of the stable. "I pray

Elsie's hiding somewhere on this farm."

He helped her mount, then jumped on his own horse. "Elsie," they called as they rode across his land. He had to concede his gratitude in having another pair of eyes helping him search. *God, please lead us to Elsie.*

His chest grew tighter with every minute that passed. The sooner he held Elsie in his arms, the sooner he'd be able to breathe again.

"Blair, look." Penny pointed to a small footprint.

Dismounting before his horse stopped, he bent down to examine the print. "It must belong to Elsie." He touched the dirt, feeling Penny's hand on his back, as she leaned over to examine the footprint, as well. "She must have travelled this way." He stood and looked into the forest.

"Did you hear that?" She stepped toward the trees, as a scream echoed through the branches.

"Elsie." The hair on the back on his neck prickled. "She cannot be that far."

Penelope grabbed hold of Blair's hand and they ran into the forest calling her name. "We're coming." She looked about, trying frantically to see the little lass. "I hear rustling." She pointed to where she had heard the sound.

From behind some densely packed trees, a woman's voice shouted, "Elsie?"

"Cindy?" Blair dropped Penelope's hand and ran to his sister. Her eyes were feral as she scampered from tree to tree, holding the trunks to keep her wobbly legs from collapsing.

"Blair." Cindy grasped his arm. "I heard people screaming, 'Elsie'. My daughter? Is she alive?"

"Aye." He held his sister.

Penelope hugged herself to keep her tears from falling, as tears streamed down the woman's cheeks. "I thought she was dead. I thought my husband killed her. He tried to kill me," Cindy's voice shook. "I couldn't face the world without Elsie in it," she snuffled into his shirt.

His eyes misted. "Your husband's dead. He cannot hurt you or Elsie anymore. You're safe here." He hugged her, then pulled back. "Elsie's missing though and we must find her." His sister nodded, swatting away tears. "Can you walk well enough to accompany us?"

"Aye, of course. I must find my daughter."

"Then hold my hand and lean on me for support."

"I shall be fine. Just find her."

He took Cindy's hand and shot a look at Penelope. She thanked God for the change in Cindy. *Now God, please help us find Elsie.*

"Elsie," she began shouting once more as they moved through the trees. "Please create some noise so we can locate you."

"I'm here," Elsie's voice whistled through the air. Penelope's eyes darted back to Blair's. With an arm around his sister, they ran toward Elsie's voice.

"Keep speaking, Elsie," he shouted, several feet to Penelope's right.

"I shall try," Elsie responded, then began to talk incessantly. Penelope laughed with relief.

"She is the most darling chatterbox." He grinned at Cindy.

"Blair, she's down there." Penelope dropped onto the ground above a ditch. "Elsie, are you hurt?"

"Nay. But I cannot climb out." She tried in vain to grip the dirt wall.

"Be patient." She smiled down at her. "We shall pull you out."

"Thank—" her eyes widened "—Mama?" she muttered.

"Aye." Cindy dropped to her knees, crying. "'Tis me."

"Mama." Her tears and expression turned from shock into happiness.

"Elsie, take my hand." Blair reached his arm into the ditch and a grunt escaped him as he pulled his niece to safety.

"Oh, Elsie." Cindy grasped for her daughter, as he fell back and let Cindy fuss over her child.

Relief and happiness swept over Penelope. Her moistened eyes met

Blair's as she approached him. "God answered our prayers."

"Aye." He smiled as he watched his family reunite.

She sat next to him. She wanted to hug him, but after the events of to-day, she knew she couldn't, and she trembled. Having the man she loved despise her, hurt more than any punishment he could wield as a warden.

"We ought to return to the house." He rose. "I shan't wish my sister to exhaust herself."

"Of course." She followed his lead.

"I shall send for the doctor to-morrow," he spoke his thoughts aloud. "Cindy must be examined. A doctor must proclaim her well." His face contorted into a mixture of deep thought and concern. "But, behold her, I suspect she's more than fine."

"Uncle Blair, can my mama sleep in my room to-night?" Elsie asked from inside her mother's arms.

"If she wishes," he answered, with a look to his sister.

"I never wish to be separated from you again." Cindy cupped her daughter's chin, then hugged her.

The grin on the little lass' face lightened Penelope's heart. "You're welcome to any of my nightgowns," she offered.

"Thank you." Cindy flashed her a smile.

"Aye, thank you," Blair stammered.

Did he not think she possessed any generosity or goodness? She bit her bottom lip. How would she ever convince him that she wasn't a terrible person?

"Blair, may I speak with you?" she asked when they neared his home.

"Nay." He glanced at her, but his eyes didn't even connect with hers before they darted back to his sister and niece, who walked ahead of them.

Her feet stumbled. She hadn't expected such a hostile rejection.

"It shan't do to have you fall." He grabbed her arm and steadied her. But not even a hint of a smile crossed his lips, and he continued to avoid her eyes.

"Thank you," she murmured, and hugged herself after he swiftly removed his hand. Did she repulse him?

"Elsie, " Halcyon ran to her. The relief on Mickey's face said everything. "Ye don't know how worried we've been."

"I'm sorry," Elsie mumbled. "But I found my mama and she's never leaving me again."

"Wonderful." Halcyon's eyes flew from Cindy to Blair.

"They're both fine," he answered her look of concern.

Halcyon smiled and tears glistened her eyes as she took Cindy's arm. "Allow me to help ye."

"Thank you." Cindy never released Elsie as they all headed for the stairs.

Blair stopped Mickey. "Meet me in the kitchen in half an hour."

He dipped his chin. "I shall just make sure yer sister gets up these stairs soundly." Mickey trailed behind the women.

Blair and Penelope remained below watching their ascent. She sucked in a breath, hesitating before she spoke, "I understand your not wishing to speak with me. But I must ask, do you expect me to sleep upstairs to-night or do you wish me locked up with my brother?"

He faced her, and his eyes tore into hers, completely devoid of their usual softness. She looked away, unable to stomach the disgust and hate that looked upon her. But she couldn't fault him. She had betrayed his trust.

"'Tis been a long day." He rubbed the back of his neck. "You offered my sister one of your nightgowns, I expect after you fulfill your promise you shall retire to bed?"

"I shall." She searched his eyes, hoping to see forgiveness or some small bit of compassion in them, but they remained distant.

"Good, because I must attend to my work." He turned and marched into his study. She longed to follow him. She wished to explain herself further, to make him understand. She stepped forward, unable to stop herself from going to him. But his study door slammed shut, and she jumped back. He didn't wish her near him. Not to-night, and certainly not ever again.

Last night he had wanted to share his troubles with her, but to-night, he could hardly look at her, let alone speak to her. Tears threatened to burst forth and she knew she only had several minutes to get Cindy a nightgown before she shan't be able to control the torrent of sadness that permeated her.

Blair rummaged through his desk for his writing instruments. He had to send a letter of explanation to Fort Niagara and another one to Cindy's doctor. But then he would go straight to bed.

His head pounded, his thoughts tangled, and his emotions bled raw. And yet, the need to pray overcame him. *Thank You, God, for giving my sister back to us.* He clasped his hands together tightly. *I shall make this right,* he promised. *To-morrow I shall speak with Pastor West about rebuilding Your church.* He let out a sigh. *I'm sorry, God.* He bowed his head, and prayed about Clyde, and everything else that troubled him, including Penny.

His eyes opened at the thought of her. He didn't believe she had set fire to the church, nor did he think she had helped Clyde and Paul escape. But then why hadn't she told him Paul was her brother?

His mind raced back to his first meeting with Penny at the church. She had been looking for someone, and now he knew who, and why she had grinned upon laying eyes on Paul.

Was situating herself close to Paul the only reason she had wished to work as Elsie's nanny? He rubbed his face with a groan. He must finally admit to himself that Penny had never returned his feelings, and she never would.

That's enough thinking, he growled at himself. No amount of thought would prove beneficial. And yet his mind continued to spin. *Sleep.* He must sleep to stop the churning. But first, he stared down at the blank pieces of parchment before him, he must write these letters. He picked up his quill pen and forced the tip to move along the pages.

Done. He folded the letters, stalked out of the room and into the kitchen where Mickey poked at the embers in the hearth. "I'm sorry to ask this of you at this late hour, and after the frightful day we've endured, but I need these letters delivered."

Halcyon had evidently overheard their conversation as she entered the room. "Ye don't mean to go yerself, do ye Mickey?" her utterance wasn't exactly a question.

"Please do find someone else. I don't mind the expense. But they do need to go posthaste." Blair held them out.

"Shan't be a problem, I know just the man for the job." Mickey took the letters.

"Thank you. One is for the doctor and the other must be sent to Fort Niagara."

"Consider them delivered." Mickey kissed his wife's cheek. "I shan't be but a moment." He shuffled to the door.

"Just be careful," she warned with love in her voice. Then she turned to Blair. "Ye've had quite a day. Sleep must be beckoning ye."

"It most certainly is. But I fear sleep may elude me. Please do obtain some rest for yourself though."

"Aye." She bustled past him. "Oh, I almost forgot. Penny asked me to give ye this." He watched as she retrieved something from one of the cupboards—the same cupboard Penny had barred him from last night. "She commissioned me to hand this to ye after the wedding." Halcyon passed him a letter.

He stared at his name written in Penny's handwriting. This must be what she hadn't wished him to see. "Thank you, Halcyon. Sleep well."

"Ye, as well." He stepped out of the kitchen and bounded up to his bedchamber. Tearing the letter open, he sat on his bed.

Dearest Blair,
I'm sorry I felt compelled to leave. Indeed, I wished nothing more than to have stayed. I shall

miss Elsie terribly. Perhaps after you read this you shall understand my reasoning. I prayed, but another option failed to present itself. I only hope that one day you shall come to understand, because I shall pray you forgive me.

He raked his fingers through his hair, unable to believe what he had read. Here he had been trying to convince Penny to stay, and she had been completely adamant about leaving. But from what he had read thus far, this letter sounded akin to a confession—one Penny probably had forgotten to burn once he had brought her back.

But even though her words stared at him, he couldn't believe she had actually planned to help Paul and Clyde escape. He was certain her love for Elsie was real. And he definitely couldn't imagine she'd agree to burn down a church. He stood, and paced the room as he continued reading.

I've been keeping a secret from you, and everyone else here, and I cannot hide it any longer. By the time you read this I shall be gone. Hence, why I asked Halcyon to present you with this after the wedding. As you read this, I shall have come back for my belongings and now be on my way to Newark. Hence, you shall know that I never kept my secret for malicious reasons. I only kept my secret to ensure my safety, as well as my brother's, because he's my secret. Your prisoner of war, Paul, is my brother, P.J.

He could hear the relief Penny must have felt in sharing her secret. He sunk down onto his bed. Here in his hands was proof that she had never come to cause trouble.

My goal in travelling to the Mohawk Valley was to tell P.J. of our father's death and to fulfill my pa's dying wish that I apologize to P.J. for him. But furthermore, I had to ascertain that P.J. was being treated

fairly. If he wasn't, I ought to
have protested his treatment, and
tried to arrange for him to be
exchanged for an imprisoned
American officer, akin to what is
done with prisoners on ships.

But then I met you. I never
expected a warden to be as
benevolent as you. And I came to
realize that even though I had
come here to protect P.J., my
presence actually put him in
danger. As I became more
intimately acquainted with you,
the risk of you unearthing my
secret grew and I feared you'd
assume I had travelled here with
the sole intention of helping
P.J. escape. And we both know
what the consequences of that
are.

He cringed. All this time Penny
had been living under a shroud of
fear. Now he understood why she had
seemed terrified when he had said he
knew her secret. She had been thinking
of this, not her letter to Jamilyn
about Lachlan and Fiona.

But I can leave now without
trepidation. I know P.J. is in
your extraordinary care. However,
I do most ardently wish I didn't
have to leave Elsie. And whilst
I'm divulging this much of
myself, you ought to know I don't
wish to leave here for other
reasons, as well.

His heart began to pump blood
harder and faster. He read her last
sentence again. Hope rose him to his
feet. It did indeed sound as if she
might reveal hidden feelings for him.
But dare he anticipate this? He forced
his eyes to focus back on her writing.
One way or another, he must know.

I never meant to come to
care for you as much as I have.
And that's another reason I must
leave. You're my brother's
warden. A courtship between us is
doomed. I could never allow you
to court me whilst I knew I kept
this secret. Like you, I believe
a marriage must be nestled in
trust. But of course I've allowed
my thoughts to run rampant.

You've never stated you possess feelings for me. And thus, before I end this letter, I beg you to please try to understand why I kept this secret from you. Please don't harbor ill feelings toward me. I do wish you to write to me. I shall pray you can forgive me and we may at least be friends.

A giddy grin spread across his face. Being friends with her wasn't his intention. And to-morrow, he would discern whether she still possessed feelings for him. And if she did, not one iota of a doubt would remain in her mind regarding his feelings for her.

nable to lie in bed any longer, Penelope dressed early and began to pace her bedroom. Blair had been extremely upset yesterday. He hadn't even wished to speak with her. And now she didn't know if she was even allowed to leave the confines of her room. She had become a prisoner, with her future resting completely on his judgment of her.

She wrung her hands, freezing when a knock sounded at her door. "Come in."

"Good morning." Halcyon entered. "We heard yer footsteps."

"Sorry, I hope I didn't bother anyone." She played with a strand of her hair, wondering if Halcyon had been including Blair when she had said we.

"Nay." She waved her hand to shoo off her distress. "But since Blair heard ye were up, he wished me to come ask ye if ye would meet with him in his study?"

She nodded, but didn't move.

"Best not to keep Blair waiting." Halcyon flung out her arm, urging her to go.

"Of course." She swallowed and gathered her courage.

"Blair's a good man, Penny." She patted her back.

"I know." She forced a smile, knowing she had been the one to bring all this trouble upon herself. "Thank you, Halcyon." She marched out of her bedchamber and down the stairs, praying the entire way that God would somehow convince Blair to have mercy on her and her brother.

Taking a deep breath, she rapped on his door. But her knuckles sent the wood swinging into the room. "Sorry," she stammered. "I didn't realize the door stood ajar."

"Please, come in. I've been waiting for you."

She stepped into his study, unsure how to interpret his pleasantness. "Shall I shut the door?"

"Aye." He rose from the chair behind his desk. "Please, sit." He motioned to the seat before him.

She searched his face as she sat, but couldn't discern a thing. And not knowing which decision he had arrived at, made breathing incredibly difficult.

"I spoke with your brother earlier." He sat back down and entwined his fingers into a ball on his desk. She shivered at how he had referred to P.J. as her brother.

"Shall I be permitted to see my brother before he's sent away or—?" She couldn't say *killed*.

"You may visit with him directly after our discussion."

"Thank you." She bit the inside of her cheek. She wanted to ask more questions, but didn't wish to press him. Upsetting him further shan't do any good.

"Penny, I asked you here because there are some things I must discuss with you."

"Blair, I understand your need not to talk yesterday, but I'm glad you're willing to do so today." She leaned forward. "If you shall allow me, I do indeed wish to explain all that occurred."

"I believe you already have."

She sat back. "Then you've already settled your mind on a course of action?"

"As much as I can."

"Please, just tell me what you've resolved to do. I didn't sleep a wink last night. I cannot seem to stop shaking and my stomach is rolling tighter then a sailor's knot." She stared down at her hands. "But I needn't concern you with such matters. I'm certain you merely wish to have me exiled from your life as fast as possible."

"I don't believe that's an option, Penny."

"Of course." Her eyes looked up to meet his. He must hand her over to his superiors. "I understand you constantly strive to do that which is right, and I don't doubt you shall behave accordingly now, but please believe that Clyde forced P.J. and I to help him escape. If he didn't threaten to kill us, we shan't have ever helped him."

"That's precisely what your brother asserted earlier when I spoke with him."

"Because 'tis the truth."

"*The truth.*" He crossed his arms, never taking his eyes from her. "Pray tell, why does telling me *the truth* pose such difficulty for you?"

She sat silent a moment. "I'm sorry I didn't confide in you that

P.J. was my brother. But you of all people ought to understand why I didn't."

His eyebrows shot up. "I ought to?"

"Aye." She sat up straighter. "You kept the secret that Cindy was alive from Elsie."

He rubbed the back of his neck. "I suppose we both acted in the manner we thought necessary to protect the ones we love."

"Aye." She squeezed her hands together hoping he understood.

"Nevertheless, Penny, I must insist you leave my house immediately."

"Immediately," she choked out his harsh word.

"Aye."

"Fine." Her eyes fell, unable to look at him any longer. "I understand."

"You must return to Pastor West's house."

"For how long?" she forced herself to ask. She had to discern as much as she could about her and her brother's futures. "Is that my punishment? Because if you believe I came here to help P.J. escape, then you must arrest me and punish P.J."

He took a deep breath and her shoulders slumped when he didn't instantly answer. She braced herself for his reply. This would be worse than she had ever feared.

"Blair McAllister, ye must come with us." Two strapping men in American uniforms crashed through the door.

Her heart beat wildly against her chest and her jaw fell open. But Blair remained calm. He took a long, deep breath before he rose. "I understand." He glanced at her, his expression one of resignation.

"I'm sorry to do this, Blair. But ye're well aware of the rules." One of the armed men pressed his lips together.

"Aye." He walked toward them. "I never fathomed 'twould occur this soon though."

"Sorry, but we have our orders."

"What orders?" She bolted out of her chair, rushing toward Blair. "What's happening?"

"Stand aside, woman. This doesn't concern ye." One of the uniformed Americans blocked her way.

"Nay, you stand aside." She tried to push past the man, but he didn't budge. "Where are you taking him?" her voice screeched, as she tried to peer around the military wall.

"He's to go into town and pay for his error."

"What error?" Her mind twirled. He had never committed an offence. He was one of the best men she had ever known.

"Wait," she shouted when Blair was led out the door.

"Listen, woman." The man blocked her view. "Blair knew he'd be punished if he ever let his prisoners escape."

"You're to punish him?" She wrapped her arms around her stomach, afraid she might hurl its contents.

"'Tis best ye remain here." The man strode out of the room, slamming the door behind him, which woke her from her sheer disbelief.

"I fail to agree," she muttered, as she ran to the door.

Rushing outside, she saw Blair already seated in a wagon and the man who had blocked her was charging toward it. "Wait," she yelled, as she ran to the wagon. "Please, you mustn't cart him away." She looked up at the men. "I shall go in his place." She clutched the sides of the wagon trying to raise herself up.

But the uniformed American pushed her hands away. "Get back in the house, woman. Ye needn't witness this." And before she could protest further, the wagon bolted forward.

She ran, trying to reach for it, determined to grab hold and jump on. But stretching her arms out, her hands fumbled through the air and she failed to secure a grip.

Panting, she stopped and rested her hands on her thighs as she looked after the wagon. The man said they were to take him into town. "Mickey," she screamed, finding the energy to run toward the stable, whilst praying Mickey dwelled within.

"Pray tell, why are ye hollering fer me?" Mickey poked his head out of a stall.

Thank You, God. She wiped the back of her hand across her moistened forehead. "I must travel into town. Now."

"In this frantic state?" He raised a brow.

"Two uniformed Americans just seized Blair." She gripped her chest, trying to catch her breath. "They said they had been sent to punish him for letting his prisoners escape."

He hastened out of the stall and began saddling up a horse. "Here, take this one. I shall meet ye there as soon as I'm able."

"Thank you." She hoisted herself up and rode off. She couldn't allow Blair to be hurt, or—it pained her to even think it—killed. She banished the thought.

Please, God, stay with Blair. Give him strength. Don't allow anything terrible to befall him. And please aid me in helping him, because I cannot accomplish this alone, I need You.

She squared her shoulders when the rooftops of the town buildings came into view. Whatever she encountered in town, she'd fight until Blair was released. And what presented itself to her looked as if she might have to fight the entire town.

She tied her horse up at the edge of the main street. She'd have ridden directly through until she found Blair, but an impassible crowd had gathered.

Dashing into the throng of people, she was certain she'd find Blair in the middle of them. "Excuse me," she scowled, pushing her way through people she didn't recognize. Had all these people come to watch a man be tortured? Didn't they know some of these punishments were brutal enough they lead to death? Or was that the enticement?

Utterly disgusted, she nudged past the last heap of onlookers. Her feet stopped as still as her heart. An enormous wooden horse had been erected in the middle of the street. Its two triangular bases, one at each end, held up a long horizontal plank of thick wood. And seated atop the lumber, as if he rode an actual horse, sat Blair.

Her stomach tightened at the sight of his anguished face. Muskets had been tied to each of his ankles. The pain from the weight of those muskets pulling down his legs must be excruciating. "Stop," she screamed, running to the bottom of the wooden horse. Those muskets could well-nigh overstretch his legs and render him permanently unable to walk, or worse, rip his legs clear off.

She stretched up on the tips of her toes and tried to untie one of the muskets. She'd heard of men who had died from injuries they had succumbed to on these torture devices and she wasn't about to lose Blair.

"Hey," one of the uniformed Americans that had apprehended Blair shouted. "Stop this instant!"

She didn't slow her hands. "Penny," Blair yelped. "You shall bring trouble upon yourself."

"It matters not." She looked up into troubled eyes. But whether their mist was due to her assistance or his excruciating pain, she knew not. "I shan't allow them to hurt you." She thanked God that one of the muskets came loose.

"'Tis not yer decision." The uniformed American seized the musket and then her arm. She struggled against the towering man, who frowned at her as he dragged her away. "I believe I spoke clearly afore whence I warned ye not to interfere." He looked into the crowd and motioned with his head for someone to aid him. She thrashed about wildly. "Please, keep this woman away from that wooden horse."

"Nothing would give us more pleasure." She looked at the man who had grabbed her right arm and then at the one who clutched her left and bit her tongue to stop herself from screaming. These were the two men who had attacked her brother outside the general store. The same men Blair had fought with, and she had waved a pistol at. "That British lover's finally getting what he deserves."

She tucked her head into her shoulder, away from the man's alcohol saturated breath. "If 'tis British people you despise, then hoist me up there as well, I'm British." She held her breath as she looked between the men.

They laughed. "We don't reprimand innocent people." The man on her left chucked her chin as if she were a child. "Blair's a warden. He failed to perform his duties. He must pay for his mistake. 'Tis for the best though. Hopefully now he shall learn his lesson. This shall teach him to treat his British prisoners in the manner they deserve."

"Make way," Pastor West's voice broke through the crowd. "What pray tell is the meaning of this?" She thanked God. Surely Pastor West could help Blair. She thrashed her arms trying to break loose, but the men only tightened their hold on her.

"See here, Pastor." The uniformed American walked straight up to him. "We have our orders to carry out this punishment and we shan't accept any interference from the church." He spat on the ground beside him. "Now return to yer congregation, ye don't have business here."

Pastor West folded his arms and stared the giant in the eye. "I shall leave once that woman is released to me." He pointed his chin in her direction.

"Actually, 'twould be of great benefit to us. Please, take her."

"Thank you." Pastor West took her hand and the two men released her arms. "I'm sorry, Blair." He looked up at him as they passed. "I shall pray for you."

"Thank you," his voice was barely audible.

"We cannot just leave him here," she squawked.

"We haven't a choice," sadness echoed in the pastor's words. "We cannot fight the military."

"Maybe you cannot, but I can." She dropped his hand and ran back to wooden horse.

"Penny, watch yourself," Blair shouted.

She turned swiftly to avoid being nabbed. *God, I need Your help.*

"Stop!" A man's voice rose above the commotion and everyone froze. "I order you to cease issuing this punishment and leave posthaste." An American officer strode confidently toward the wooden horse.

"Lachlan," she muttered, noticing Mickey followed closely behind him.

"Who's in charge?" he glared at the two uniformed Americans.

"I am," one of them stepped forward.

"Henceforth, I am." he commanded. "I've spoken with your superior."

"Aye, ye're old friends. He said ye lived in this town. Officer Lachlan McAllister?"

"Correct. Now please release Blair and dismantle that wooden horse." Lachlan glared at the men who failed to move. "Are you disobeying an order?" Both uniformed Americans shook their heads. "Good, then please proceed."

Thanking God, Penelope glanced up at the sky, her shoulders sank with relief. "Thank you, Lachlan." She touched his uninjured arm.

He winked at her. "Like you apparently, there's nothing I shan't do for the ones I love."

She smiled. Those were indeed the words she lived by. "Blair." She rushed to him after the men had untied the muskets and taken him down. He wobbled and fell to his knees.

"He can recover at my house." Pastor West held onto Blair's right side, and with Mickey taking hold of his left side, they pulled him up onto his feet. She followed with Lachlan, wishing she could be of more assistance. But she couldn't carry him. And even though the pastor's home was close, her heart splintered every time Blair's legs stumbled.

"Lie him on the sofa." Pastor West and Mickey eased him down in the parlor.

"I shall fetch the doctor." Mickey left before Blair could even utter his thanks.

"And I shall have my cook fix something." The pastor patted his shoulder and hastened to the door.

"You need rest," Lachlan observed his cousin. "But hopefully we removed you before you suffered any serious, lasting damage."

"Thank you, Lachlan. A million times, thank you." He shook his hand. "I shall be fine. Go be with your new wife. Give her my best."

"If you insist. But—"

"I'm in good hands." He reassured him.

"I shall visit later."

"Thank you." They sat in silence until Lachlan left.

Then her heart skipped when his attention turned to her. "Are you comfortable?" She busied her hands with a quilt, pulling the material over his legs. Tears streamed down her cheeks. "The fault of your infirmity lies squarely with me. If I hadn't told P.J. you had arranged to send them south, Clyde ought never to have overheard and attempted to escape."

"Nay, Penny." He moved to sit up, but pain creased his face. After a moment, he continued, "Clyde was the epitome of trouble. 'Twas merely a matter of time before he attempted an escape."

Wiping away tears that kept flowing, she seated herself on the floor beside him and squeezed his hand. "You shall be fine, shall you not?" she whispered.

"Actually—" he smirked "—that depends on you."

"Me?" she choked.

"Aye. I still have yet to explain why I wished you out of my home and back with Pastor West."

"You needn't fret about those particulars. I know you believe I travelled here to help my brother escape, and hence, you detest me."

"You're mistaken," his voice softened. "I never once said I doubted your account of events."

Her heart skipped. "You believe me?"

"Penny, you're a woman who is beyond courageous. One who'd risk her own life for someone she loves."

She nodded, fighting back tears. "I never wished harm upon you. I hoped that perhaps in time you could forgive me and then—" she couldn't finish. She couldn't tell him her dream of marrying him. He may not detest her, but he was far from loving her.

"I believe you." He smiled. "Even before I read your letter I believed you."

"My letter?" she exclaimed. "Oh, nay. With everything that happened, I completely forgot to——."

"I'm glad you forgot." He took her hand and gently pulled her closer to him. "You wrote something in your letter though that I must inquire about."

"What?" She bit her lip.

"You wrote that you had come to care for me." Her cheeks ignited. "Am I wrong in hoping you still do?" Her chin tucked into her chest. But with a tender hand, he tilted her head up. "I've come to care for you, as well. You must know you have naught to fear from me."

She rubbed her thumb over his hand. "Knowing how good a man you are, I don't."

"Good." He pulled her hand to his lips. "But can you come to care for me the way a wife does her husband?"

She gasped. "I fail to understand. You wished me to leave your house and stay with Pastor West?"

"True, but allow me to explain," he chuckled. "Your brother insisted upon that."

"P.J.?"

"Aye, he was rather adamant. And 'tis rather odd—" he grinned "—considering I'm still his warden. However, now that I'm courting his sister, he thinks he's authorized to issue me orders."

She gasped. "You're courting me?"

"If you shall permit me?" He held her gaze. "Um, I've never known you to be speechless."

"Nay." She smiled sheepishly. "But you must excuse me. I've never been confronted with an offer this dear to my heart and nearest my deepest wishes."

"Those are precisely the words I've longed to hear." He pulled her even closer. "I may have agreed to your brother's demands, but hopefully we shall only need to abide by them for a wee bit. I love you, Penelope Sherwood, and wish you to return home as my wife."

She sat up on her knees and reached her arms around his neck. "I love you, Blair McAllister."

"You've just made me the happiest of men."

"Good, because I'm the happiest of women."

"Truly?"

"Aye. Why do you doubt me?" She tried to pull away, but he gently held her close.

"Because I can think of something that ought to make you even happier."

"Impossible." Her eyebrows pinched together.

He laughed. "Perhaps if I told you I made arrangements for your brother to remain here until the end of the war, and in the meantime, I shall rewrite his parole agreement to allow him more freedom?"

Tears escaped her. "Then I stand corrected, and I must tell you I love you all over again."

"Then I'm glad I rose early this morning, because I shall never tire of hearing you profess your love for me."

"Blair McAllister, I love you," she laughed, moving closer to him.

"Penny, I prayed from the first day I met you that God had sent you to me."

"And I've prayed that God would somehow find a way for us to be together."

"Then we had better not waste any more time. If God meant for us to be together, who are we to stand in His way?"

She shrugged and he leaned over. Finally, she was free to kiss him. She cradled his face in her hands, as his fingers travelled up her back and into her hair.

"I've wanted to do this since I first beheld you." He pressed his lips to hers.

Nearly breathless, she grinned. "I hope 'twas worth the wait?"

"You tell me." He kissed her again and she laughed. "Elsie shall be ecstatic once she learns her princess nanny is to be her aunt."

"And this time I shan't argue my unknown lineage, because you do indeed make me feel as if I were a princess."

He grimaced. "Then I must apologize, for that has never been my intention."

She squinted. "I fail to understand?"

"Until now, I've been prohibited from truly courting you. Hence, why you merely feel akin to a princess," he smirked. "But now that nothing prevents me, be prepared to trade your princess' tiara for a queen's crown."

"My lord doth please me exceedingly," she chuckled.

He pulled her into a kiss that made her sigh with pleasure. "That, my beautiful queen, shall be my life's work."

Guarded Hearts

Please Enjoy the other books in the

HIGHLAND HEARTS IN THE AMERICAS

Series

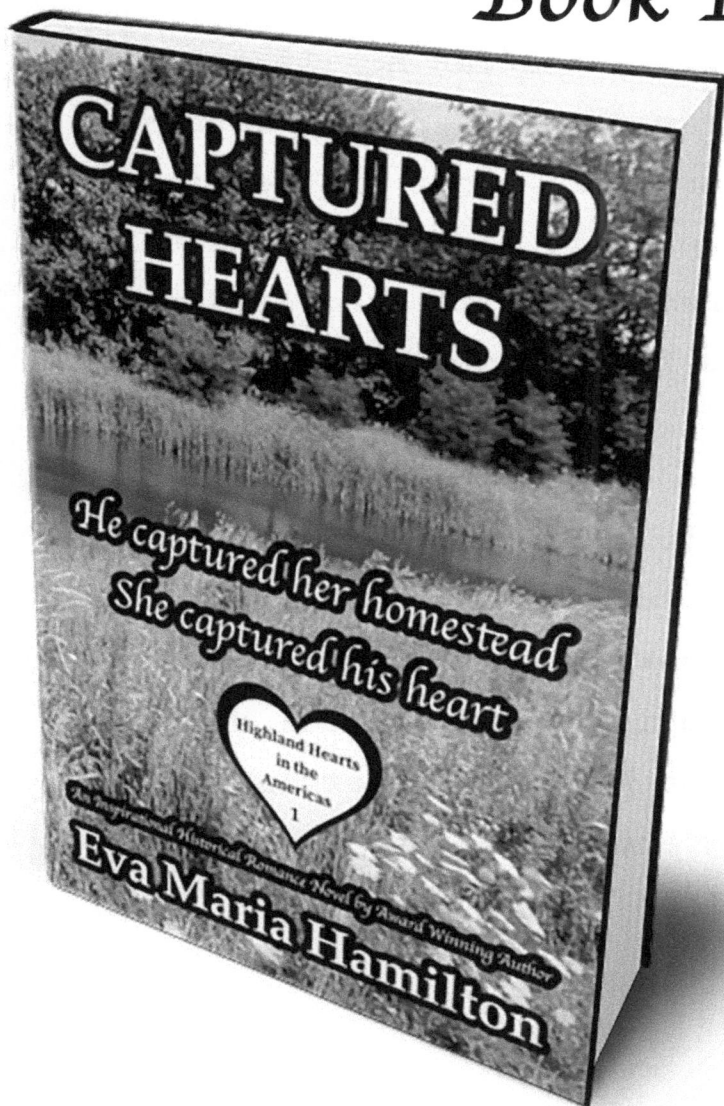

Book 1

CAPTURED HEARTS

He captured her homestead
She captured his heart

Highland Hearts
in the
Americas
1

An Inspirational Historical Romance Novel by Award Winning Author

Eva Maria Hamilton

On separate sides of the War of 1812, Lachlan McAllister and Fiona Robertson are reunited. But will their old feelings be rekindled in time to save Lachlan's life and lead them to a future together?

With guest appearances from beloved Highland Hearts characters; Captured Hearts begins a new series: Hearts in the Americas, starring the grandchildren of the couples from Highland Hearts.

CAPTURED HEARTS

He captured her homestead
She captured his heart

Highland Hearts
in the
Americas

1

An Inspirational Historical Romance Novel by Award Winning Author

Eva Maria Hamilton

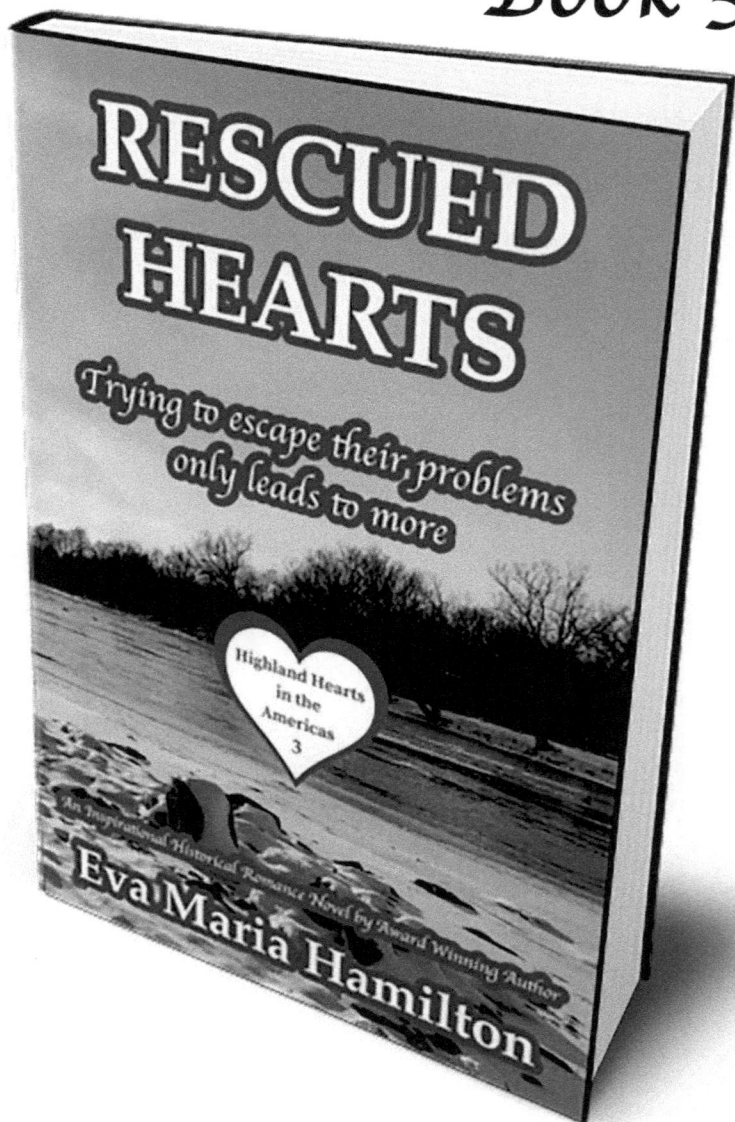

Book 3

RESCUED HEARTS

Trying to escape their problems
only leads to more

Highland Hearts
in the
Americas
3

An Inspirational Historical Romance Novel by Award Winning Author

Eva Maria Hamilton

Jamilyn West switched homes with a friend to get away from her problems. But one man is not willing to let her go. Cole Munro has secretly travelled into enemy territory during the War of 1812 to ensure Jamilyn's safety. But his presence puts both their lives in jeopardy. And even though he has no desire to return to their hometown either, they may have no other choice but to risk their lives in an escape that leads them directly to the trouble they left behind.

RESCUED HEARTS

Trying to escape their problems
only leads to more

Highland Hearts
in the
Americas
3

An Inspirational Historical Romance Novel by Award Winning Author

Eva Maria Hamilton

Dear Reader,

I hope you enjoyed Guarded Hearts!

Penny and Blair both have a love for their families that is truly wonderful to witness. Now that they're together, it's amazing how strong a force they must be.

I pray that you always know love and have the support of wonderful people in your life.

If you liked Penny and Blair's story, please leave a review, they mean the world to me.

And please also connect with me.

I look forward to meeting you and staying in touch!

Sincerely,

Eva Maria Hamilton

About the Author

Eva Maria Hamilton spent years studying people from all different areas of academia and brings that understanding of the human condition into each of her written pieces. An advocate for lifelong learning, Eva Maria Hamilton studied in both Canada and the United States, earning a diploma in Human Resources Management, a Bachelor of Arts degree in Psychology, an Honours Bachelor of Arts Degree in History, and a Master of Science in Education. She homeschooled her oldest daughter who is now in university, and still homeschools her youngest daughter, along with their two collies, while acting as Co-CEO in her Co-founded business, TestLauncher.

Eva Maria Hamilton is the author of Highland Hearts, a Love Inspired Historical novel published by Harlequin. Her novel, Highland Hearts:

- **Won 2nd Place in the Heart of Excellence, Reader's Choice Contest - Historical Romance Category**

- **Won 2nd Place in the Heart of Excellence, Reader's Choice Contest - Inspirational/Traditional Romance Category**

- Was an **Inspirational Series Finalist in the 2013 Gayle Wilson Award of Excellence**

Eva Maria Hamilton is also the owner of Lilac Lane Publishing, which has published a series of Jane Austen Colouring & Activity Books.

Her book, The Ultimate Collection of Jane Austen's Colouring and Activity Books: With More Than 240 Activities And Over 250 Illustrations from 1875-1906:

- Won the 2024 International Impact Book Awards.

Connect with the Author

To discover other books
Eva Maria Hamilton
has published, or soon will,
please visit her online:

EMAIL:
EvaMariaHamilton@gmail.com

FACEBOOK: Eva Maria Hamilton

FACEBOOK: Lilac Lane Publishing

X / TWITTER: @HamiltonEvaM

LINKEDIN: Eva Maria Hamilton

AMAZON.com: Amazon Author

AMAZON.ca: Amazon Author

LILAC LANE PUBLISHING:
www.LilacLanePublishing.com

WEBSITE:
www.EvaMariaHamilton.com

The Award Winning Book That
Started It All

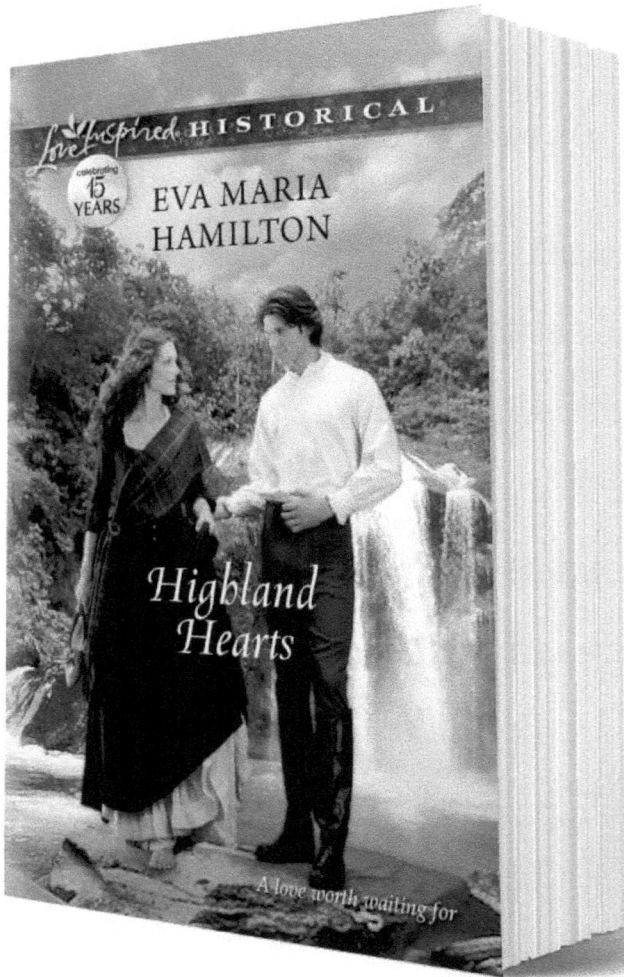

Love Inspired HISTORICAL

celebrating 15 YEARS

EVA MARIA HAMILTON

Highland Hearts

A love worth waiting for

Highland Hearts

Scotland 1748

The Battle of Culloden is over,
but one Highlander's fight has
just begun — Logan McAllister
survived years of indentured
servitude in the Americas to
reach this moment. Now he's
returned to Scotland, ready to
redeem the secret promise from
Sheena Montgomery's father —
that his years as a servant
would earn him Sheena's hand in
marriage. But when he arrives
home, he learns that Sheena's
father has died, his contract
has been lost — and Sheena is
engaged to another man.

"A good story that shows the lifestyles and prejudices that prevailed in 18th-century Scotland..."
Romantic Times

"Fascinating Scottish Romance...

Can't wait for more from this author."
5 Star Reviewer

"A great story about an interesting period...I look forward to reading more books by this new author."
5 Star Reviewer

"I found this to be a wonderful book...Highly recommend this book."
5 Star Reviewer

"An edge of your seat romance! Excellent! Loved it!"
5 Star Reviewer

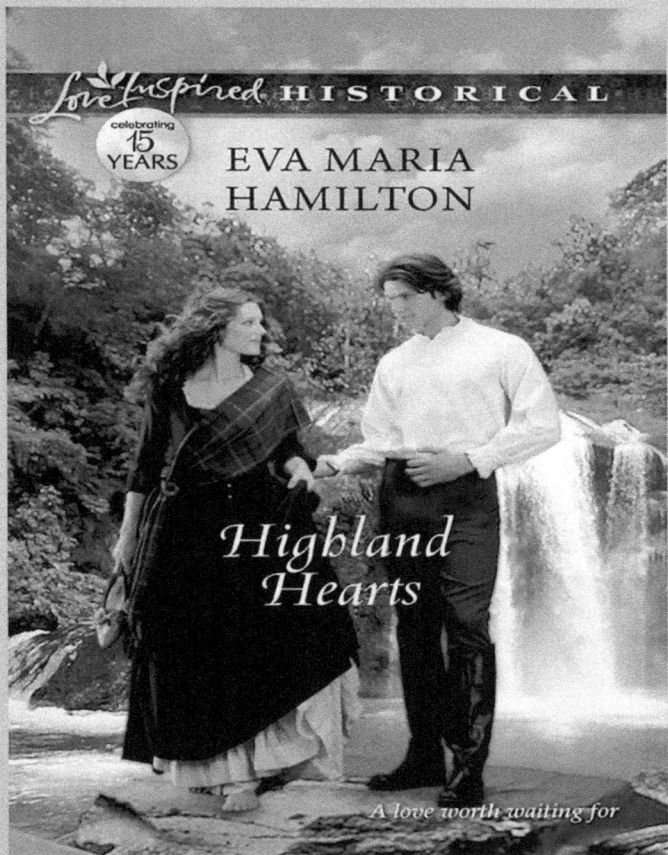

Please Also Enjoy:

DISINHERITED LOVE

A Short Inspirational
Historical Romance Story
from Award Winning Author

Eva Maria Hamilton

England 1795
An elopement in Gretna Green
seems like the perfect solution,
but for these star-crossed lovers
trouble finds them first

Disinherited Love

Lily Chrisson and Lord Gavin Mackenzie hail from very different classes; a serious problem for those in love during Regency England. And yet, they're en route to secretly marry in Gretna Green. That is, until she discovers the truth. Torn apart, his determination wars with her principles, and family with even more secrets emerge in this redeeming short story.

Jane Austen's
Pride And Prejudice
Colouring & Activity Book

By Eva Maria Hamilton

Featuring Illustrations from 1895

Step into the world
of Jane Austen!

Immerse yourself in colouring 40 illustrations from the 1895 edition of Pride and Prejudice.

Enjoy 40 activities, such as Matching Characters to Quotes, Search Words, Anagrams, and more.

Have fun in the Regency Era!

"...If you are a fan of Pride and Prejudice you will love this book. The illustrations are wonderful and the activities are engaging."
5 Star Reviewer

**Rated
5 Stars
On
Amazon**
★★★★★

Jane Austen's
Sense And Sensibility
Colouring & Activity Book

By: Eva Maria Hamilton

Featuring Illustrations from 1896

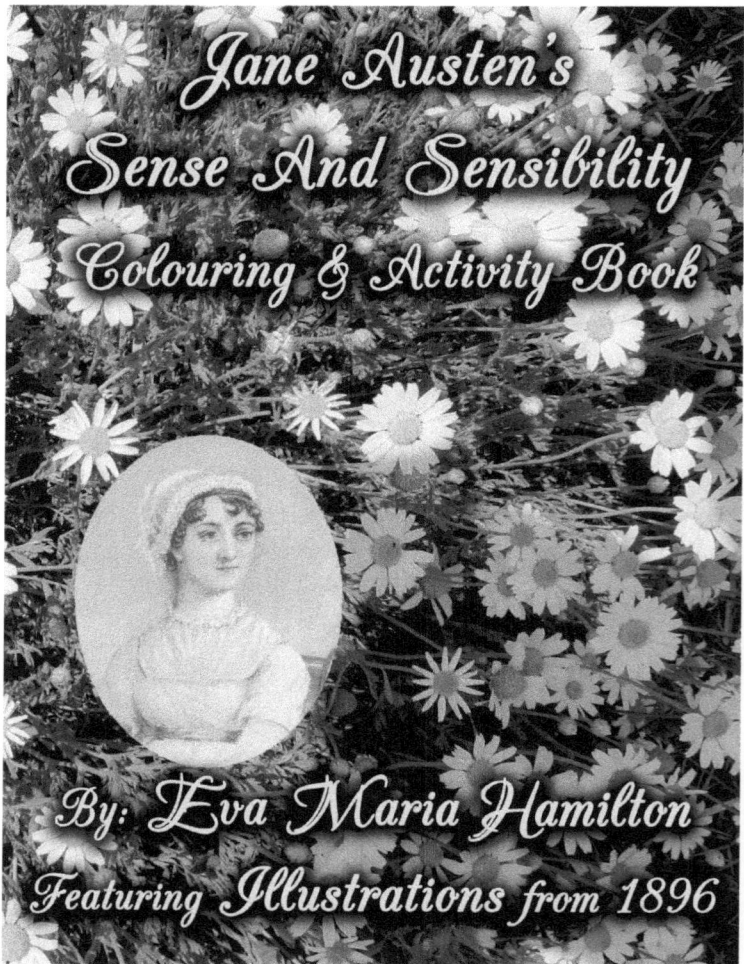

Step into the world
of Jane Austen!

Immerse yourself in colouring 40 illustrations from the 1896 edition of Sense and Sensibility.

Enjoy 40 activities, such as Matching Characters to Quotes, Search Words, Anagrams, and more.

Have fun in the Regency Era!

Rated
5 Stars
On
Amazon
★★★★★

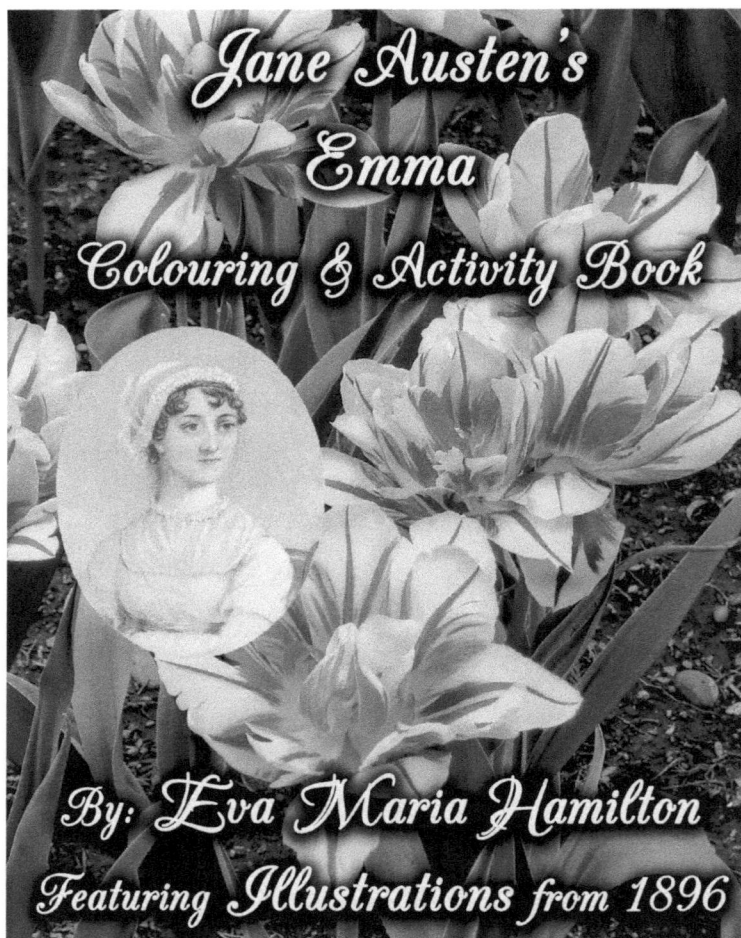

Jane Austen's
Emma
Colouring & Activity Book

By: Eva Maria Hamilton

Featuring Illustrations from 1896

Step into the world
of Jane Austen!

Immerse yourself in colouring 40 illustrations from the 1896 edition of Emma.

Enjoy 40 activities, such as Matching Characters to Quotes, Search Words, Anagrams, and more.

Have fun in the Regency Era!

"Beautifully presented... Lovely as a gift."
Reviewer

Rated
5 Stars
On
Amazon
★★★★★

Jane Austen's Persuasion

Colouring & Activity Book

By: Eva Maria Hamilton

Featuring Illustrations from 1897

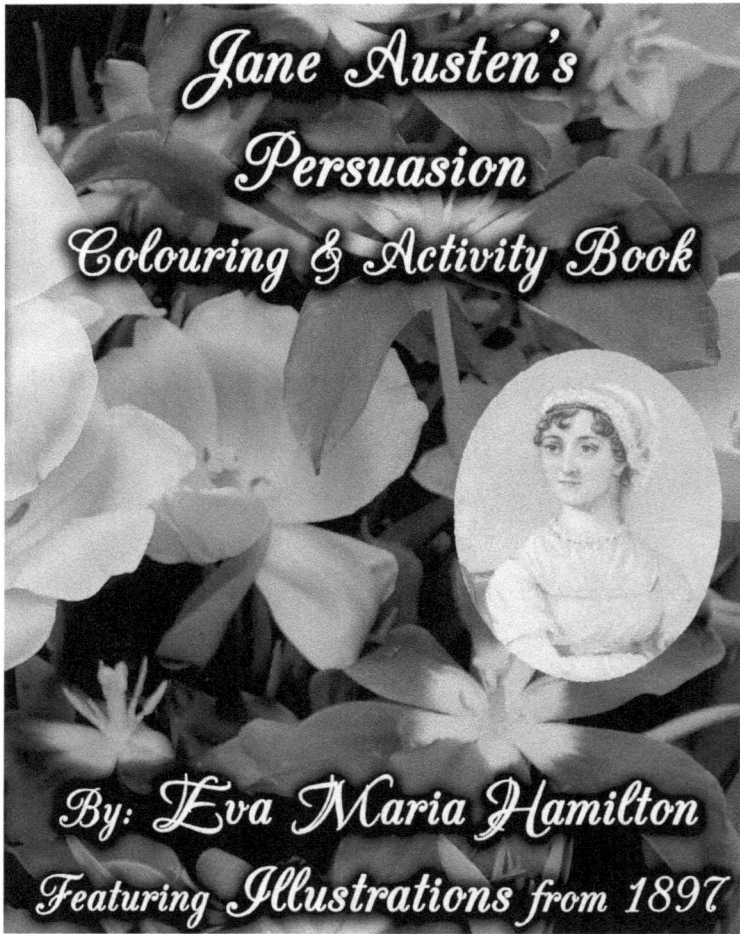

Step into the world
of Jane Austen!

Immerse yourself in colouring 20 illustrations from the 1897 edition of Persuasion.

Enjoy 20 activities, such as Matching Characters to Quotes, Search Words, Anagrams, and more.

Have fun in the Regency Era!

"Very educational...
Very beautiful."

Reviewer

Rated
5 Stars
On
Goodreads

★★★★★

Jane Austen's Mansfield Park
Colouring & Activity Book

By: Eva Maria Hamilton

Featuring Illustrations from 1897

Step into the world
of Jane Austen!

Immerse yourself in colouring 40 illustrations from the 1897 edition of Mansfield Park, plus 7 bonus illustrations from the 1875 edition.

Enjoy 47 activities, such as Matching Characters to Quotes, Search Words, Anagrams, and more.

Have fun in the Regency Era!

Rated
5 Stars
On
Amazon
★★★★★

Jane Austen's Northanger Abbey Colouring & Activity Book

By: Eva Maria Hamilton

Featuring Illustrations from 1897

Step into the world of Jane Austen!

Immerse yourself in colouring 20 illustrations from the 1897 edition of Northanger Abbey.

Enjoy 20 activities, such as Matching Characters to Quotes, Search Words, Anagrams, and more.

Have fun in the Regency Era!

Rated
5 Stars
On
Amazon
and
Goodreads
★★★★★

The Ultimate Collection

All 6 Books in 1 Plus More

of Jane Austen's

Colouring & Activity Books

Pride & Prejudice

Emma

Persuasion

Sense & Sensibility

Mansfield Park

Northanger Abbey

Plus Bonus Illustrations, and Activities From Her Other Writings:
Sandition, Lady Susan, The Watsons, Letters, and more.

By: Eva Maria Hamilton

With More Than 240 Activities
And Over 250 Illustrations from 1875-1906

The Ultimate Collection
of Jane Austen's
Colouring and Activity
Books, including:
Pride and Prejudice,
Sense and Sensibility,
Emma,
Mansfield Park,
Persuasion, and
Northanger Abbey.

Plus bonus
illustrations
and activities
from her other
writings:
Sandition,
Lady Susan,
The Watsons,
Letters,
and more.

With more than
240 activities
and over 250
illustrations
from 1875-1906!

9 781068 990724